Done Crabbin'

Also by Gilbert Byron

These Chesapeake Men (1942)

Delaware Poems (1943)

White Collar and Chain (1945)

Chesapeake Cove (1953)

The Lord's Oysters (1957)

The Wind's Will (1961)

Chesapeake Duke (1965)

Sunbathing with the Professors (1982)

The Cove Dweller (1983)

The Sight of the Marsh Hawk (1985)

GILBERT BYRON

Done Crabbin'

 ## Noah Leaves the River

A Sequel to *The Lord's Oysters*

The Johns Hopkins University Press

Baltimore and London

The Johns Hopkins University Press
701 West 40th Street
Baltimore, Maryland 21211
The Johns Hopkins Press Ltd., London

The paper used in this publication meets the minimum
requirements of American National Standard for
Information Sciences—Permanence of Paper for Printed
Library Materials, ANSI Z39.48-1984.

Library of Congress Cataloging-in-Publication
Data will be found on the last printed page of
this book.

Contents

	Acknowledgments	ix
	Author's Note	xi
	Prologue	1
1.	Captain Cable's Big Maria	3
2.	Mrs. Peasy Got an Answer	15
3.	Poor Emily	21
4.	Too Proud to Fight	30
5.	That Old Red Stutz	38
6.	Spitting Nails	45
7.	She Did, Did She?	51
8.	Sweeter than Violets	61
9.	We All Screamed	76
10.	All God's Children	87
11.	New Girl	99

12. Grandpappy's Final Hour   104

13. In Search of Arbutus   116

14. On Dead Man's Curve   125

15. To Make the World Safe   133

16. Bird in Hand   141

17. Water Boy   154

18. Moving to Baltimore   167

19. Meet the Pope   177

20. Bird on Wing   188

Acknowledgments

Some stories in this book have appeared previously through first rights arrangements with their publishers. The author wishes to thank these editors for first using his work: H. Hurtt Deringer, editor of the *Kent County News*; Betty D. Rigoli, editor of *Chesapeake Bay Magazine*; Harold D. Jopp and H. R. Ingersoll, editors of *Shoremen: An Anthology of Prose and Verse of the Eastern Shore*, Tidewater Publishers; and Kathy Simmons, editor of *Upper Shore Shopper*.

My special thanks to Arlene W. Sullivan, assistant to the director of the Johns Hopkins University Press, for her guidance and encouragement.

To Scotti Oliver, curator of the Maryland Room of the Talbot County Free Library, for research and suggestions.

To Phyllis Davis, who typed the original manuscript; and last, but not least, to my former student and friend, Jacques T. Baker, Jr., who as my literary assistant has been with us all the way.

⟨🐚⟩ Author's Note

This new book continues the stories I began in *The Lord's Oysters*, resuming at the point that the coming of the automobile and the outbreak of World War I began to fragment the island-like remoteness of the Eastern Shore. Noah Marlin says good-bye to his idyllic boyhood. The stories are told in the colloquial language of the young Noah.

◄◙► Prologue

In *1914, the town* was already more than two hundred years old, having flourished in its favorable location on a broad river that flowed into Chesapeake Bay. One street that stretched along the river was a treasury of eighteenth-century mansions that once were the homes of the town's leading merchants and shipowners. These men were proud of their English heritage, but they resented paying taxes that were levied by a distant English Parliament. In 1774, a group of townsmen went aboard the brigantine *Geddes* that was carrying a cargo of tea subject to a tax, and tossed all of the tea into the Chester River.

The town was also the county seat with a row of offices across from the ancient court house, where the lawyers took care of their clients' business during the day and played poker at night.

In 1914, when the Germans invaded Belgium at the start of World War I, the first automobiles were attacking the remoteness of the Eastern Shore. A town ordinance ridiculed those "gasoline buggies" and required that they stop on meeting a horse-drawn vehicle.

The town was a seat of culture with an ancient liberal arts college that stood on a hill overlooking the river. Each summer a floating theater pushed up the river to give the citizens a week of live drama in contrast to the motion pictures that were presented in the town hall. Chautauqua raised its big tent for another week of culture.

The annual county fair provided horse racing and oriental dancing girls for the sporting element. Intoxicating liquors were plentiful until outraged citizens led by the WCTU marched to the polls and banned the sale of alcoholic beverages in the entire county.

Several churches provided for the religious needs of its citizens, but since colonial days, when horse racing and gambling were rampant, the town had enjoyed a racy reputation. In 1786, a famous Methodist preacher, the Reverend Francis Asbury, wrote in his journal: "I preached at night at Chestertown. I always have an enlargement in preaching in this very wicked place."

In December 1914, young Noah Marlin, an inhabitant of the town, was on his way home from school, when . . . but let him tell his own stories.

1

🐚 Captain Cable's Big Maria

It was Friday afternoon, just two weeks before Christmas. I was on my way home from school when a big flock of wild geese flew over our town. The geese were low and not heading south. They were honking wildly. I figured they had been shot at and were looking for a safe place to feed and spend the night. The geese followed the river upstream; the Chester widens again about two miles above the bridge, where Morgnec Creek flows through a broad marsh. Captain Cable keeps his schooner, *Bohemia*, there at Buckingham Wharf, during the coldest weather. Mama attended a two-room school nearby, but that's another story.

When I got home, Mama was all excited about something. "Good Lord, Noah," she said. "Look out in the woodshed and see what your father has brought home from the river."

I opened the door carefully, remembering the time Dad trapped two giant snapping turtles. A number of wild geese and wild swan were hanging from the rafters; I counted eleven geese and ten swan. The white swan were much larger than the geese.

"Where'd Dad get them?" I asked.

"He ran up the river to Buckingham and bought them from Captain Cable. The Captain must have got into a big flock with his long gun."

The mention of Captain Cable's long gun reminded me that he was a market hunter during the cold months. Dad sold some of his kill to commission merchants in Baltimore. While we were talking Dad came home. I heard him whistling and knew that things were going his way.

"I telephoned the merchant in Baltimore," he said. "He's taking all of them. I'll ship them tomorrow morning on the *B.S. Ford.*"

"You can't get rid of them swan too soon for me," Mama said. "One of them nosy game wardens might pay us a visit."

"How'd Captain Cable shoot all those geese and swan, Dad?" I asked.

"He bushwacked them with his big gun, Big Maria," Dad said. "It only took one shot."

I had heard stories about these big guns the market hunters used, but I had never seen one. They were as big as small cannon. Sometimes when I was outside at night, I heard a loud boom that couldn't have been made by a 12-gauge shotgun, or even a 10-gauger. I figured it was one of the market hunters. At the time, the only gun I owned was an air rifle.

"Have you ever seen Captain Cable's big gun, Dad?"

"Only once when I caught him by surprise," he said. "The Feds have been rounding up the big guns for years; they're agin the law, but so far they haven't found his Big Maria."

"Do you know where he hides his big gun?" Mama asked.

"If I did, I wouldn't tell you, or nobody. The Captain won't even tell his own wife where he hides his big gun. She's real jealous of Big Maria."

"Boy, I'd like to shoot that gun," I said.

"You don't hold Big Maria to your shoulder. Not unless you want her to kick your arm off. She rests in chocks in the skiff he uses to hunt wildfowl."

"How big is she?" I asked.

"Big Maria stands ten feet tall and weighs about two hundred pounds."

"I'd really like to see that gun," I said.

"I'm running up the river to Buckingham tomorrow morning to see if the Captain has shot any more wildfowl," Dad said. "Why don't you come with me. Captain Cable might show you his big gun."

"I don't want Noah out on the river when the water is so cold," Mama said. "He might fall overboard."

"I'll be real careful, Mama," I said.

"It will be good for him to get some fresh air in his lungs after being inside all week," Dad said.

"All right," Mama said, "but you will have to dress warmly. I'll get your mackinaw out of the moth balls and air it."

We were out of bed Saturday morning before the sun was up. Mama had mixed buckwheat batter and placed it in back of the stove to rise. There's nothing I like better than buckwheat cakes and molasses for breakfast. Mama even gave me a cup of coffee.

"This will warm you up," she said.

"There's nothing like a cup of coffee to get your blood circulating," Dad said, pouring himself another cup.

We slipped on our hip gumboots. Mama gave me a couple of hot biscuits to put into the pockets of my mackinaw.

"These will keep your hands warm for a while," she said. "If you get hungry, you can eat them."

The sun was coming up as we walked to the cove. I could see the outline of the great heron that was fishing in the shallows off the point. Dad says the same heron has been fishing there since he was my age. I guess he thinks the point belongs to him. The tide was low enough for us to wade out to the bateau, which was moored to a stake. Dad knelt down before the big wheel of the one cylinder engine and worked it back and forth, loosening the cold oil and building up compression inside the cylinder. He squirted some gasoline into the petcock in the head of the cylinder and turned on the timer. When he turned the big wheel, it kicked backward as the gasoline was ignited by the spark plug, but the engine didn't start. Dad had to prime the cylinder a couple of times before the engine started with a roar that must have awakened a lot of people who live along Water Street. I was in the bow ready to drop the mooring line. We ran out of the cove and up the river toward Buckingham. The wind on my face was cold; I turned away from it to watch the town fade in the early morning mist. Along the shore, a narrow band of white looked like a lace collar. It was the first ice of the season.

The mist hung low over the water, so low that it hid a large flock of canvasbacks until we were only a few feet away from their lookouts. The ducks called out in fear and flew farther up the river, toward Morgnec Creek and its broad marsh. As we approached Buckingham, a large flock of wild geese and swan was feeding off the mouth of the creek. The waterfowl saw and heard our bateau; they swam into the creek, disappearing behind the tall marsh reeds.

"Captain keeps his ducking skiff in the creek," Dad yelled above the roar of the engine. "He paddles out of the creek just before dark to bushwack them."

Ahead of us, the schooner, *Bohemia*, was moored to Buckingham Wharf. We ran in alongside the wharf, and Dad cut off the engine so as to have enough headway to coast past the schooner. I jumped to the wharf and slipped our bow line around a piling.

Smoke was rising from the pipe above the cabin of the *Bohemia*, so we knew that the Captain was aboard. He came up on deck.

"That engine of yours is the loudest one on the river," he said. "I heard you long before I saw you."

"It's not as loud as your big gun, Captain," Dad said. "I heard you fire last night, just before dark, and figured I'd come up river and see what you killed. I brought Noah along."

Captain Cable looked at me for the first time. He squinted his eyes and I felt like he was looking right through me. "You're George's boy, I can see that," he said, "but you're not turning out the way I figured you would."

"Noah does well with books," Dad said. "His mama is planning to send him to the college on the hill. We want him to have a better life than we have had."

"What's wrong with your life, George?" the Captain asked. "You've done the things you wanted to do. Nobody has more than that."

"Sometimes the pickings are lean," Dad said. "We want Noah to wear a white collar every day."

"My boys are going to be schooner-men, just like their pop," the Captain said. "I don't know what would happen if a waterman gets a college education. I hope Noah don't turn out to be one of them educated fools."

"How'd you make out last night, Captain?" Dad asked.

Captain Cable led us down the ladder into the hold of his schooner. Hanging from nails in the deck beams were a large number of geese, swan, and canvasbacks. I counted fourteen geese, ten swan, and twelve canvasbacks.

Dad whistled. "You really got into them."

I've never seen Captain Cable smile, but this time he managed to grin. "Not bad for one shot, eh? What will you give me for them?"

Dad looked at the waterfowl more carefully and I knew he was about to bargain. "It's Saturday and I can't ship them until Monday morning. They might spoil on the way to Baltimore."

"We had our first ice last night, George, you know that. Besides wild game tastes better if it hangs a day or two before you cook it."

"I can't be certain if I have a buyer until I telephone the merchant," Dad said.

"Since when have you had any trouble selling wildfowl just before Christmas, George?" the Captain said, shrugging his shoulders. "All right, if you don't dare to take a chance, I'll carry them across the river to Crumpton."

Dad took a plug of chewing tobacco out of his pocket and offered it to Captain Cable before cutting himself a strip. "You know I like to gamble, Captain," he said. "I'll give you twenty dollars for these wildfowl you killed with one shot. That's not bad pay for ten minutes work. That's more than the president of the U.S. makes."

"Twenty dollars," Captain Cable snorted, and I thought he was going to swallow his cud. He spit a long stream into the bilge. "You'll get fifty dollars for them and maybe more."

"I may," Dad said, "but don't forget I have to pay the freight. If they go bad on the way, where will I be?"

"No deal," the Captain said.

"Twenty-five dollars," Dad said, spitting into the bilge.

The captain spit again. "All right, George," he said, "providing you bring me ten pounds of number-four shot the next time you run up the river. The last time I bought any shot, that game warden, Puss Dameron, was hanging around the hardware store. He's still trying to find my Big Maria."

"Will do," Dad said and pulled out a large roll of bills. Mama says Dad pads his roll with a wad of newspaper.

"Good Lord, George," Captain Cable said, "if I'd known you was loaded, I'd bargained for more."

Dad grunted. "Noah has been asking questions about your big gun, Captain. How about showing him Big Maria."

"You know how I feel about my big gun, George. The less folks know about Big Maria the better it is."

"Noah wouldn't tell anybody," Dad said. "He's as tight-mouthed as a January oyster."

"I hope not," the Captain said. "Anybody who told anybody about my Big Maria wouldn't have long to live in this world."

He gave me his fiercest look and walked over to the long centerboard that takes the place of a keel when the schooner is sailing. The board is housed in a wooden case about twenty feet long. It is raised and lowered by a long rope that runs through a hole in the deck and is fastened to a cleat on the mast. Now the board was raised.

Captain Cable moved to the forward end of the centerboard case and raised a loose board. He reached inside and pulled out Big Maria. The Captain is a powerful man, but it was all he could do to move his big two-hundred pound gun. He leaned it against the centerboard case.

"Here she is," he said, pausing to catch his breath. "Did you ever see a gun to match Big Maria, Noah?"

"No, sir," I said, moving over to where I could touch Big Maria. The gun had been cleaned recently. It was longer than the six-pounder cannon that stands on the Brewster farm.

"What size shell does it use?" I asked.

"Big Maria is a muzzle loader with a two-inch bore. I load her with black power and shot."

I touched the trigger. "How do you fire her?"

"With a cap," the Captain said and touched a hole in the top of the barrel. "I prime her here."

I couldn't take my eyes off of Big Maria.

"My daddy had her made by a gunsmith who lived in Lancaster, Pennsylvania. He called her Big Maria after his mother-in-law. Puss Dameron has been trying to find her for years. Last winter, Puss and another warden camped in the marsh all night trying to catch me. Old Zeke Marlin saw them and fired his gun three times; that's the signal we use when the wardens are on the prowl, so I stayed home."

"We'll keep your secret, Captain," Dad said, and I nodded.

Captain returned his big gun to its hiding place. He helped Dad and me carry the wildfowl to the bateau. When Dad turned the wheel the engine was still warm—it started the first time. Captain tossed our bow line aboard and we ran down the river. We were home in time for lunch.

That afternoon our gang played football until Mickey got kicked in the nose. It bled and wouldn't stop so we stopped for a while.

"I heard your father's bateau early this morning, Noah," PeeWee Sumner said. He's new in town. His father is so rich that PeeWee can't play football with us so we let him referee.

"He went up to Buckingham to buy some wildfowl," I said. "I went with him."

PeeWee is also the nosiest boy in town. "We had canvasback for supper last night," he said. "Who sold you the game?"

"Captain Cable," I said.

"I heard his big gun last night, just before dark," Ric said. "Kroooom! it sounded more like a cannon than a shotgun."

"It's longer than the cannon on Mr. Brewster's place," I said.

"You mean you've seen Captain Cable's big gun?" PeeWee asked, and the boys drew closer.

"Pop had a big gun once," Ric said. "The game wardens caught him using it. Took the big gun and fined him a hundred dollars."

"I'll betcha the Captain showed you his big gun," PeeWee said. He'd make a good lawyer. "Didn't you see it?"

Mama tells me that I must always tell the truth and on Sundays our rector warns us that we must never lie. PeeWee had me and he knew it. And I knew what Captain Cable would do to me if I told anybody where he hid it, but everybody knew he had the big gun, and PeeWee had so many things that we didn't have, I had to best him this once.

"Sure he showed it to me," I said. "The Captain could hardly lift it out of where he hides it."

If I had told the kids that I had suddenly inherited a million dollars, they wouldn't have been more impresseed.

"Where does he hide it?" PeeWee asked, still prying.

"That's one thing I can't tell you. Captain would finish me off."

"He'd blast you with his big gun and cut up what was left of you for crab bait," Ric said.

"If you were in the courtroom and the district attorney asked you, you'd have to tell," PeeWee said.

"You're not the district attorney," I said. "I'm not telling nobody, never."

For once Ric came to my aid. "I don't blame you."

"We wouldn't tell anybody," PeeWee said.

"I'm not telling nobody," I said. "I'll go to jail first."

Mickey's nose had stopped bleeding. We played football until it was time for supper.

While we were eating, Dad mentioned that he had sold the wildfowl to the merchant in Baltimore. "When you go to church tomorrow, you'd better pray for cold weather, Evaline," he said.

"Why don't you come to church with us and add your prayer, George?" Mama said. "It might help."

"I feel so cooped up in church, like I might be in jail," Dad said. "I feel closer to the Good Lord on the river."

"That's silly talk," Mama said, "and it's not good for Noah to hear such nonsense."

I knew what Dad was talking about. When we were river running the bateau, on a sunny day, with the blue sky overhead and the blue water under our boat, it sometimes seemed that we were in paradise. And when you are out on broad water in a little boat, you really have to believe that somebody is watching over you.

On Sundays I go to church three times: in the morning I go to the regular services with Mama—the young rector is not as long-winded as the older one; in the afternoon, I go to Sunday School; and in the evening, there is the children's choir that the young rector has started. Anybody knows that is too much for anybody. Dad says it will mark me for life.

Anyway, when I came home from Sunday School, Mama was visiting with Miss Lizzie, across the street, so I found my air rifle and slipped out the back door so Mama wouldn't see me. I vaulted over the back fence and ran down to the cove where Dad keeps his bateau. In the marsh I found a glass bottle that had been left there by the high tide. I tossed it into the water; it would make a good target.

The beach was deserted. I filled the magazine of the rifle with fifty beebees and aimed. I missed. It took me three shots to hit the bottle, which was rocking up and down on the waves.

"Good shot!" a voice called and I turned to see a man I had never seen before. He had moved up on me as silently as a cat.

Mama and Dad have always told me not to speak to strangers, but this man was well dressed. He looked like one of the touring preachers who held revival services at the Methodist church.

"Want to give me a shot?" the stranger asked.

Even Mama says that I'm an easy touch. I handed my rifle to the stranger. The way he drew it up to his shoulder told me that he knew a lot about guns. He hit the neck of the bottle with his first shot. The bottle filled with water and sank.

"You need a bigger gun," the stranger said, returning my rifle. "Something like a 12-gauge hammerless shotgun."

"Do you sell guns?" I asked.

"You might say I deal in guns. I collect them."

"I borrow my grandfather's double-barrel sometimes," I said. "It is very old and was made in England."

"Right now I am looking for a bigger gun, one that is ten feet long and weighs two hundred pounds," the stranger said. "Last night when I was dining on wild goose, a little bird told me that you might help me find it. If you can, I'll make you a Christmas present of the best shotgun money can buy."

I could feel the hair standing up on the back of my neck. "I don't know what you are talking about, Mister," I said. "Anyway, it's time I went home."

The stranger moved closer and placed his hand on my shoulder. "You are Noah Marlin?"

"Yes, sir," I said. "I'm Noah, and the way I figure, you're a game warden."

The stranger took a firmer grasp of my arm. I don't know what would have happened, but lucky for me I heard a man whistling, and only one man could whistle like that. It was Dad coming down to the cove to check his bateau. As he emerged from the marsh, he was carrying the grapnel to the bateau; he had spliced a new line on the anchor. It was swinging to and fro, its sharp flukes glistening in the sun. Dad can really toss his grapnel. I've watched him spear turtles and snakes. Once he snagged the body of a college boy, after he broke through the ice on the river and drowned.

Dad took one look at the stranger, swinging the grapnel as if he were about to throw it. "Has this man been bothering you, Noah?" he asked.

I didn't want to see a fight, especially on a Sunday. Somebody might get hurt, somebody might go to jail.

"We were just talking, Dad," I said.

"Do you know who this man is?" Dad asked.

"I figure he is a game warden."

"You figured right," Dad said. "This is Puss Dameron; you've heard me mention him."

Dad turned again toward the game warden. "I want to talk to my son alone, Puss," he said. "If you know what's good for you, you'll start moving."

The stranger disappeared into the marsh as silently as he had arrived. I guess that's why everybody calls him "Puss."

I never did find out who told Puss I knew where Captain Cable hid his Big Maria.

2

🐚 Mrs. Peasy Got an Answer

Sometimes I think the Meekins boys are the luckiest ones in town. They go down the river in their rowboat whenever they want to and carry cat rifles. They never go to church and only go to Sunday School once a year. In December they go to get their names on the roll just before Christmas so that they can get a stocking of candy and an orange. Ralph Meekins says the Methodists have the best candy. He ought to know.

Mama makes me go to church and Sunday School every Sunday. That's bad enough, but now a new rector has come to our church and he has started a young people's choir that sings during the evening services. Three times in one day is too much.

The day Mrs. Mooney, the organist, had the tryouts I was as hoarse as an old crow but it was no use.

"My voice is changing, Mrs. Mooney," I said. "It would spoil everything if I squeaked in the middle of a hymn."

"That's all right, Noah," she said. "Soon you are going to have a beautiful tenor. You come to rehearsal Thursday evening at eight o'clock. I'm going to have cake and candy for refreshments after we finish practicing."

"Yes, ma'am," I said, though it didn't seem Christian to be luring us with sweet stuff.

The only one of us boys who escaped was Ric. He was taken with chicken pox the first week our children's choir practiced.

The girls like to sing in the choir more than us boys. I think they like the idea of getting out Thursday nights, because afterwards we play Hide and Seek. It was spring and the peepers were singing in the marshes. It's a lot of fun to play Hide and Seek in the spring. And Mrs. Mooney could make good chocolate caramels and cake. Chocolate is my favorite.

Everything went along fine with the choir. We sang the *Magnificat* and the *Nunc Dimittis* after the first and second readings of the Scriptures, and three other hymns. We did have a little trouble when it came to choosing a boy to carry the cross as we marched in and out of the choir and to light the candles during communion. Most of us thought the members of our choir should elect the acolyte, but our rector appointed him. It turned out to be Lester Sumner. He is well suited to light the candles. When he was only seven years old, he set his home afire playing with matches. His parents are well-off and every Sunday Mr. Sumner comes to church and puts a five dollar bill in the collection plate. Anyway, the young rector likes to please everybody, so he selected Lester. He says, "Eeny, meeny, mini, mo" while he is putting out the candles. That's the kind of boy he is.

Everything went fine until we started practicing on some new music for Easter. Mrs. Mooney said that the anthem needed a bass soloist.

"I don't know what to do, Noah," she said. "Couldn't you sing bass for us this one time?"

"That's one thing I can't do, Mrs. Mooney," I said. "My voice is getting squeakier every day."

"Do you know of any boy we might get to join our choir who could sing bass? He wouldn't even have to belong to our church."

I knew of someone but I was scared to tell her. "There's one boy who could do it, Mrs. Mooney. If I tell you, will you tell anybody I told you?"

"I won't tell anybody," she promised.

"Ricard has a good bass voice," I said. "His voice has finished changing. You ought to hear him sing the number about the bells of the sea, in his woodshed. He can hit the lowest notes, just like Billy DeRue does in the Minstrel Show."

Ric never sang much in school, but he had a place in the woodshed with pictures on the wall from the *Police Gazette*. He could really sing bass in his woodshed.

"Ricard belongs to our church doesn't he?" Mrs. Mooney asked. "How did he miss joining our choir?"

"He had chicken pox that week."

"I'll speak to his mother," she said.

"Please don't say I told you," I said.

On Thursday Ric came to choir practice and seemed to have a good time. Mrs. Mooney said the choir was lucky to have found a boy who was mature enough to sing bass. Ric liked that, and he also liked playing Hide and Seek after choir practice—he always hid with Dora Tilghman. But the second Sunday after he joined the choir changed all that.

Most of us go to church early and stand around in back of the organ kidding the girls. The congregation can't see us, and Mrs. Mooney never bothers us as long as we are fairly quiet. That night, Simon, who pumps the organ, hadn't arrived yet and the girls had taken their places in the choir. Us boys had the place to ourselves.

"Where does the rector keep the wine, PeeWee?" Ric asked

Lester Sumner. He doesn't like to be called that nickname, even though he is smaller than the rest of us.

"Wouldn't you like to know?" Lester said. "I take a couple of swigs every time we have communion."

The door in back of the organ had been left open, and the steps that led up to the pipes were down.

"Where do those steps go?" Ric asked. He is always interested in mechanical contrivances.

"That's where Simon goes to dust the pipes," I said.

All of us at one time or other had sneaked up those steps and looked through the peephole that is in front of the organ. You can see everybody in the church, but they can't see you.

"What's up there?" Ric asked.

"Why don't you go up there and see for yourself?" PeeWee said. "Everybody else has been up there, even the girls."

"I don't want to get into any trouble in church," Ric said, gazing through the door and up the steps.

"You must be scared," PeeWee said. "I dare you to go up there. I double dare you."

That settled it. "You can't double dare me," Ric said, stepping through the door and climbing the steps. He disappeared.

Just then Mrs. Mooney came around from the front of the organ. "You boys take your places in the choir," she said, and noticing the organ door open, she closed it. It clicked shut and it was locked, too. Simon came in through the back door and began to pump wind into the organ. I wondered if Ric felt the breeze.

"Where's Ricard?" Mrs. Mooney asked. "I thought I saw him earlier this evening."

"He must have sneaked out the back door and ran off," PeeWee said.

We took our places and opened the hymnals to the first

hymn, "From Greenland's Icy Mountains," and I could hear Simon puffing as the organ swelled to his pumping. I wondered if Ric was cold. When Mrs. Mooney played the verse over, it sounded like she had missed a couple of notes. She looked in Simon's direction, but he was doing his part. He always rubs snuff and dozes through the sermon, jumping whenever the preacher raises his voice. But he was pumping hard then.

When we started to sing, the organ sounded like it was choking to death. I wondered what Ric was doing to those pipes. At the end of the second verse, the organ let out a shriek like a fire whistle and Mrs. Mooney almost jumped off the organ bench. After that she just pretended that she was playing.

During the first Bible reading I listened to see if I could hear Ric moving around, but he didn't even make a squeak. "Maybe he's asleep," I thought.

But when the rector finished the reading, and the organ started to play the *Magnificat*, it was certain that he was awake. Being mechanical, Ric must have turned the screws that tune the organ and work the valves. It was terrible—I mean the organ—and sounded like the circus calliope playing, "There'll Be a Hot Time in the Old Town Tonight." Mrs. Mooney must have realized that the organ was out of human control. She stopped. After we finished singing, the rector said that something had happened to the mechanics of the organ, and that we would dispense with the singing for the rest of the service. While he was talking, I could hear Ric moving around in the organ, getting more and more restless.

The rector started to read the second lesson from the Bible. He was doing all right as he chanted:

"Hear my voice, O God, answer me."

"Help me down from here," a voice answered, coming from the top of the church, by the big chandelier. The rector stopped reading and looked toward the ceiling. Everybody else was look-ing toward the ceiling; all of them had heard Ric, but we boys and girls were the only ones who knew who it was.

Old Mrs. Peasy, who always stoops and crosses herself before entering the pew, crossed herself and raised her eyes, expectant. I guess she had been waiting for years, hoping Some-body would answer the rector's request.

The rector looked around him and must have decided that he had only heard one of his congregation.

"Hear my voice, O God, answer me," he called again.

"Dammit, let me down from here," Ric called, and this time he was louder and angry.

Mrs. Peasy went down on her knees followed by most of the congregation. It isn't every Sunday the congregation gets an answer. Ric's voice was like the God in the Old Testament, mighty and angry.

When Ric started rattling the organ door and shouting, Simon began to wave his hands. By this time, Mrs. Mooney must have figured it out. She found the key to the organ and unlocked the door.

Ric bounded out and dashed through the back door, but Simon was ahead of him. I could hear the steel plates on Ric's heels ringing on the brick pavement. They had to get a man from Baltimore to fix the organ.

3

🐚 Poor Emily

Whenever the showboat came up the river, after it had gone we talked of giving a show of our own. We could never decide whether to give a western melodrama or something like "Peck's Bad Boy." The girls weren't interested. Anyway, it's more fun to play outside in the spring, running and hiding games before it's warm enough to play baseball.

One Saturday morning we were playing Run, Sheep, Run. Me and Ric were the sheep and the rest of the fellows were the wolves. The pack gave us five minutes start; that was enough. The sheep fled around the corner, across fields and along the cinderpath road down the neck. A plowed field slowed us, but by the time we reached the woods, everything was quiet.

I stopped to pick an Indian moccasin flower, a pink one. Dad says that there are yellow ones, too, but I've never found one.

"Only sissies pick flowers," Ric said, trying to start a quarrel.

I didn't notice him. I was listening to a bird singing, deep in the woods. It was calling, "secret, secret, secret."

When we came to the woods' road Ric stopped and pointed

to the ground. "Somebody has been in here with a horse and carriage," he said.

The tracks of the wheels were fresh in the soft earth. We stood listening. The bird had stopped singing. A single brown leaf drifted out of an oak tree. When the leaf touched the ground, we heard it. It was that quiet.

"What are you scared of?" Ric sneered

"I saw two tramps this morning. They were coming this way."

"Tramps don't ride. Let's follow and see."

We didn't have far to go.

Ric was in the lead and spied the black carriage first.

I felt better because I knew that rig. It belonged to Doc Bellers; he's yanked more teeth than anybody in our county. That dentist can hurt you when he gets you in his chair, but he can't touch you outside. Besides, Doc Bellers has a wooden leg, and even worse, he's an old bachelor. You know how old bachelors are—they can shout and warn you, but that is about all they can do. That wooden leg doesn't keep him from drilling and prying and yanking, but he can't do much else.

We watched the carriage. It was moving slowly away from us, slower than a soft crab, the horse grazing and the reins on the dashboard. Maybe Doc Bellers likes to pick wild flowers, I thought, or more likely he's been digging sassafras root for his spring tea. Then we began to hear noises in the carriage, first what sounded like a woman giggling, followed by Doc Bellers's laugh, the way he does when he tells you it won't hurt much, just before he picks up the forceps. Ric nudged me. He was grinning and rolling his eyes like he knew what was going on. When the carriage began to shake, Ric almost fell down laughing.

I couldn't figure it out, not until Emily, she's Doc's old mare, stopped grazing and turned her head. Emily could see what was going on inside the carriage, and whatever it was, she didn't like it. The old mare lifted her upper lip like Rags used to when I petted the cat. Emily snorted and ran away. Doc Bellers yelled and reached for the reins, but he couldn't slow Emily down. The woods' road has a twist in it, and when Emily made the curve, we could see Doc's lady friend. Only one female in town had yellow hair the color of cornsilk in May, and that was Miss Bertie Parker, our fifth grade teacher. Mama said she must dye it. But it was nice to have a teacher with pretty yellow hair and a soft voice who smelled sweet. Now we saw her, hair and all, and Miss Bertie looked up in time to see us.

"What d'you know about that," Ric said. "She must be hard up."

I nodded. Maybe I didn't understand all the facts of life, but I had a pretty good idea why Emily ran away; poor Emily, she had been pulling Doc Bellers's carriage ever since I could remember. He drove her to his office in the morning, and there she would stand all day, waiting to take him home again.

Doc lived by himself without even a housekeeper, and ate his meals at the boarding house where Miss Bertie and some of the other school teachers stayed. He fed Emily whenever he thought about it. And now Emily had to carry Doc's lady friend—poor Emily! Only somehow it didn't make sense. Doc must have been fifty or more and there was his wooden leg. I'd never seen it, but he limped, and whenever I ran after a horse and wagon, Mama would call to me and ask if I wanted a wooden leg like Doctor Bellers. Dad said the boys in school used to stick pins in it and Doc would yell out like it was his real leg, just to bother their teacher.

"I'll betcha we'll pass now, even if we don't do another lick of homework," Ric said.

"What d'you mean?"

"We'll hold it over her. If she doesn't pass us, we'll tell."

"I'm passing anyway," I said.

"I'm failing arithmetic and you know what that means. They can hold me back if they want to."

"Doc Bellers might torture us if we tell," I said. I could imagine myself going to him to have a small filling, and then he would strap me in his chair—it wasn't worth the chance.

"I hadn't thought of that," Ric said. "Ma told me yesterday that I'd have to go to see him as soon as school is out."

That decided us. We wouldn't tell anybody what we had seen or what Emily might have seen. On the way home, we didn't see any of the wolves—they must have given up the chase.

Mama stopped me at the kitchen door. "Didn't I tell you to be home at three o'clock?" she demanded. "Where have you been?"

"Yes, ma'am," I said, taking off my muddy shoes.

"Where have you been all afternoon?" she asked again.

I told her everything, all about being chased by the wolves into the woods, but I didn't mention seeing Doc Bellers and Miss Bertie. Then I remembered the flowers in my shirt.

When I gave Mama the bouquet, she smiled, sweet-like, even though the blossoms were creased and worn. "You've got to be careful when your menfolks bring you flowers," she said. "Are you telling me the truth?"

"Yes, ma'am."

"Don't you go into the woods again with Ric or anybody else," she said. "Boys do strange things in the woods, especially when they run wild in the spring."

Dad was resting on the couch, and we must have disturbed him. I heard the springs squeak. "What do you know about what boys do in the springtime woods, Evaline?" he asked.

"Why don't you stop fussing with Noah and let me rest?"

Mama flew into him.

After supper, she filled the wash tub and I took a bath before going to bed. I was awfully tired from all the running and walking and was asleep when a closing door awoke me. I could hear Sister Helen; she's Ric's mother.

"Lawrence was ready to lick Ricard about ruining his shoes. He was showing Ricard the strap when he confessed."

"I don't believe it," Mama said. "Noah looked me straight in the eye, and he didn't tell me about it."

"I've told you before, Mama, and I'll tell you again. Noah is innocent looking but he is also full of guile."

Mama changed the subject. "You know Doctor Bellers has a wooden leg."

Sister Helen laughed.

"Wait until George hears about this," Mama said.

"Well, if Doctor Bellers wants a wife, at his age he could do worse," Sister Helen said.

"It won't be a happy marriage, May and December, not counting the wooden leg," Mama said. "Do you suppose Noah is still awake?"

"He's probably listening to everything we say."

For a moment I thought Mama had started for the stairs, but she must have changed her mind. Their voices became fainter and I could only hear a word now and then—I must have dropped off to sleep again.

Mama was after me the next morning, even before I had finished breakfast.

"This is the Lord's Day, Evaline," Dad said. He never went to church but he liked to argue.

"That sounds strange coming from you," Mama said. "Noah won't be twelve until July. I must know what he saw. Did you see what Ricard saw, Noah?"

"Yes, ma'am."

"He answered you," Dad said. "Now let's have some more flapjacks."

"You're both alike," Mama said. "Noah, did you see inside Doctor Bellers's carriage?"

"No, ma'am."

"Did Ricard see?"

"No, ma'am."

"Then who did?"

"Emily."

Dad laughed. "I'll bet old Emily was plenty jealous. Doc has been driving that mare for more than ten years."

"Maybe nothing happened," Mama said, "but it's scandalous for a female teacher to go riding in the springtime woods with a bachelor."

"How about with a married man?" Dad asked.

Mama didn't answer that. "I'm going to keep Noah home from school until this matter is straightened out. He won't learn anything good from such a teacher."

"What's that have to do with arithmetic, Mama?" I asked.

Dad laughed but Mama didn't. "You speak when you are spoken to, young man."

But she let me go to school Monday morning. All of the kids were talking about Miss Bertie and Doc Bellers and what Emily may have seen. The fellows cornered me in the cloakroom and asked all about it, but I wouldn't say anything.

It was plain that Miss Bertie knew that we knew. While we were reading out loud, Ric came to a sentence about a horse. He stopped for a second, and Miss Bertie's face turned as red as a beet. But the girls seemed to like Miss Bertie even better than before. During recess they put their arms around her.

When Doc Bellers passed me at noon in his carriage, I

couldn't help staring to see if Miss Bertie was beside him. She wasn't, but I had to look. Emily was picking up her feet smart-like, and you could see that she was glad to have Doc alone again. Then I noticed that the old mare was wearing blinders—that must have been Doc's way of telling Emily to mind her own business. Doc saw me looking and touched Emily with his whip. She jumped and started down the street like it might have been the racetrack at the county fair. It was all Doc could do to keep her from running away again.

The men standing in front of Mr. Billy Mac's store laughed when Emily kicked up her heels.

"That old mare is really jealous of Doc Bellers," Mr. Leary said.

"Poor Emily has been carrying him hither and thither for a long time," said Mr. Brewster. He's a lawyer and likes to argue. "You can't blame Emily."

"She couldn't have seen much, anyway," Mr. Leary said. "Doc can't do much with that wooden leg."

"I wouldn't be so sure of that," Captain Cable said. "Do any of you remember Iky, my old toll gander? You know how wild a gander is around mating time; he'll jump into a dog, or a horse, or anybody who interrupts his love-making. Well, this colored fellow I had took a team of mules past where Iky and his mate were building their nest. I had warned the fellow, and told him to take the mules another way, but you know how boys are. Well, sir, Iky flew right into the mules and started to beat the lead one with his wings. The mule kicked Iky, and for a while it looked like the end for my toll gander. When he came to, one of his legs was all torn up, so I took my axe and chopped it off at the first joint. After it healed, I made Iky a wooden leg, and doggone if he didn't live and make love for ten more years. Every year he mated with the same goose."

"That's not the same," Mr. Leary said. "Doc Bellers ain't no toll gander."

"It has a bearing on the question," said Mr. Brewster.

I was late getting home for lunch. "Did that woman have the gall to come to school?" Mama asked.

I nodded my head.

"I've a great mind to take myself out to that school and give her a piece of my mind."

"You'll do nothing of the kind," Dad said.

He doesn't tangle with Mama unless he has to.

"Since when did you have such a great interest in the romantic, George?" Mama asked. "It sounds like you are taking their side."

"Judge not lest you be judged," Dad said. "It might do Doc Bellers a lot of good to have a pretty young wife. Maybe he'd be more gentle with them forceps."

"You ought to have been a lawyer, George," Mama said. "It doesn't help Noah to hear such talk."

She didn't visit the school but several other mothers did. After they left, Miss Bertie cried. The girls put their arms around her again, but we boys couldn't do anything. We couldn't even behave ourselves, and when Miss Bertie let us out after keeping us after school, there was Doc Bellers and Emily, waiting to take her home or wherever they were going.

When Mama heard about that she exploded. "You're not going back to that school as long as she teaches the fifth grade," she said.

That night I added a prayer for Miss Bertie.

Dad complained and said the truant officer would arrest him, but Mama said maybe that would make him get a steady job. Nobody can do anything when Mama puts her foot down.

The next morning she kept me busy around the house, but

in the afternoon, I slipped away to the river. The fish wouldn't bite so I went home. Mama and Miss Lizzie were talking in the parlor.

"They were married by a justice of the peace late yesterday afternoon," Miss Lizzie said. "Mrs. Tilghman told Mrs. Kennard and she told me. Well, I hope they'll be happy."

"Doctor Bellers is lucky to have such a pretty woman to love," Mama said.

"I wonder what Doc Bellers will do with Emily," I said.

Mama saw me for the first time. "What's that got to do with it?" she demanded. "You're going back to school tomorrow, young man."

I did. We had a substitute teacher for the rest of the year and you know how substitutes are. We had a lot of fun.

Poor Emily! Only a few days after Doc and Miss Bertie got married, he sold Emily to Greenley's Livery Stable and bought a yellow Dodge roadster, the color of Miss Bertie's hair.

4

🐚 Too Proud to Fight

It *was Friday*—school was over for the week. After supper Dad gave me a quarter and asked me to go uptown and get him a pack of Sweet Caporal cigarettes and a copy of the *Evening Bulletin*. The newspapers came in on the train; I went down to the railroad station to be sure to get one. Since the war in Europe started, the newspapers had been selling out fast.

When I passed the town hall, the big clock in the tower began to strike seven, so I ran the rest of the way to the station, expecting to hear the whistle of the Bullet when it blew for the crossing by the mill pond. We called the train the Bullet because it was so slow. But it was late. When I reached the station a lot of people had gathered to buy newspapers. Ric was there.

"Did you hear the latest?" he asked. "A German sub has sunk another ship."

"Was it ours?" I asked.

"I don't think so," Ric said. "Mr. Elliot got the news on the telegraph. It was an English liner, but a lot of Americans were aboard."

Everybody was listening for the whistle of the Bullet.

When the wind was right, we could hear her blow for Worton; that's three miles away and the last stop before ours. We are at the end of the line.

I was thinking of asking the station master how late the train was when she blew for the crossing at the edge of town. Soon we heard the steam hissing after the engineer applied the brakes to slow her down. Mr. Elliot lowered the gates at the crossing and began to ring the bell to clear the tracks. The Bullet passed the station house, snorting and panting, and came to a stop. Rip Parr was waiting with a cart to get the newspapers.

Mr. Green, the conductor, was the first to step down from the passenger coach. He was followed by several drummers carrying sample cases; they climbed into the hack that carried them to the hotel.

I was lucky to get a newspaper that evening and ran most of the way home. Even though it was getting dark, I could read the headlines:

GERMAN SUBMARINE SINKS LUSITANIA

More than 1000 Passengers Lost

It was a warm evening. Mama and Dad were sitting on the front porch when I got home.

"You might think you were a race horse," Mama said. "Sit down and catch your breath."

Dad read the headlines. "Good Lord!" he said, "The *Lusitania* was one of the biggest ships afloat, and also one of the fastest."

"Somebody ought to do something about those German submarines," Mama said. "It's not human to drown women and children like those Germans are doing."

"Let's go inside and read about it," Dad said.

Mama lit the big nickel lamp with the white shade and Dad read the newspaper out loud. Usually, it was the other way and Mama read from books or magazines.

"More than a thousand persons are missing," Dad said, "and that includes one hundred Americans."

"They should have stayed home where they belonged," Mama said.

"Here are the main facts," Dad said. "The Cunard liner, *Lusitania*, was torpedoed by a German U-Boat at 2 P.M. (Eastern Standard Time) on May 7th about ten miles off the coast of southern Ireland after crossing the Atlantic. The luxury liner listed to one side and sank in eighteen minutes. The *Lusitania's* passengers and crew totaled 1,917. Many lifeboats carrying women and children were smashed while being lowered from the davits. A first count of survivors shows that more than one thousand persons are missing."

"It's as bad as the *Titanic*, Mama said. "Do you remember that, Noah?"

"That must have been 1912," Dad said. "Fifteen hundred persons were drowned when the liner hit an iceberg."

"Our teacher told us that the *Titanic* was unsinkable," I said.

"The British must have thought that the *Lusitania* was fast enough to run away from the German subs," Dad said, "but a U-Boat must have waited for her."

"I don't know what the world is coming to," Mama said, "and since my folks were almost all English, I can't feel neutral like President Wilson says we should all be."

"One of your grandmothers was Dutch," Dad said.

"That's not the same as German," Mama said. "One of your grandmothers came from Hamburg."

She and Dad started to argue about their families, so I found the book I was reading. It was the first of a new series about the Boy Allies, and like Mama, it favored the English.

The newspapers on Saturday and Sunday had more details on the sinking of the *Lusitania*, including a drawing of the vessel as she went down. I like to draw pictures of boats, but mine are schooners with their sails full of wind. The *Lusitania* was almost eight hundred feet long, with four stacks, and was launched in Glasgow, Scotland, in 1907. Just as Dad said, she was very fast, and that same year she was launched, set a new record crossing the Atlantic. On her best run across the ocean she averaged 25.85 knots an hour. That was fast on land or sea in 1915.

When I went to school on Monday, all the kids were talking about the sinking of the *Lusitania*. Our substitute teacher, Miss Agnes Weems, was even younger than Miss Bertie. She was young enough to be interested, too, and asked Dora, who was keeping a scrapbook of clippings about the war, to read what she had about the *Lusitania*. Dora's father was the only person in town who subscribed to the *New York Times*. She had one clipping that the other papers didn't have. It was a warning placed in the newspaper by the Imperial German Embassy on May first, the day the *Lusitania* sailed from New York, and read:

> Notice: Travelers intending to embark on the Atlantic voyage are reminded that a state of war exists between Germany and her allies and Great Britain and her allies; that the zone of war includes the waters adjacent to the British Isles; that, in accordance with formal notice given by the Imperial German Government, vessels flying the flag of Great Britain, or any of her allies, are liable to destruction in those waters and that travelers sailing in the war zone on ships of Great Britain or her allies do so at their own risk.
>
> IMPERIAL GERMAN EMBASSY, Washington, D.C., April 22, 1915

That announcement by the German Embassy started a big argument.

"The German Kaiser can't tell us Americans where we can travel or on whose ships," Ric said.

But some of the girls thought Americans should stay out of the war zone and not risk bringing us into the war.

Dora read another clipping that told about how the British had declared a blockade of the North Sea and stopped several American ships.

"Stopping ships is not the same as sinking them," Ric said, and that made sense to most of us boys. But most of the girls supported Dora.

While we were arguing, the noon dismissal bell rang. We were so interested that none of us heard it, and continued talking until Mr. Manning rapped on the door to see what was the matter.

After lunch the debate started all over again in history class. "Why doesn't President Wilson declare war on Germany?" Hicky asked. "I'll betcha if Teddy Roosevelt was president, he would."

Miss Agnes knew the answer to that question. "The Constitution of the United States gives only Congress the power to declare war," she said.

The Constitution was in the appendix of our American history textbook, but none of us had ever read it. Now we had a good reason and found the clause that gave Congress the power to declare war, and other clauses saying that Congress could appropriate money to raise and support armies, a navy, and to organize and call out the National Guard.

"Why does Congress have so many powers?" Erny asked.

"The Congress is elected by the people of all the states," Dora said. "It represents all the people."

"The president is elected by the people, too," Ric said.

"Not directly," Miss Agnes said. "The voters in the different states vote for electors, with the number of electors each state has depending on its population. Then the electors cast their ballots for the presidential candidate."

"It's not a good idea for one man to have the power to declare war," Dora said. "That's too much power to give one man."

"By the time Congress meets and acts, it might be too late," Ric argued.

The way we were interested, everyone, even our teacher, forgot our history assignment in the textbook about the Spanish-American War. Then I remembered.

"Look what happened when the *Maine* was sunk in 1898," I said.

"That was different," Dora said. "The *Maine* was an American war ship and 260 of our sailors were lost."

"She was blown up by a mine," Erny added.

That sent us to our history textbooks again, where we read that President McKinley had sent a message to Congress asking for the power to intervene in Cuba. Four days later Spain declared war on the United States.

We would have liked to have continued our history class for the rest of the afternoon, but it was time for arithmetic. That quieted us for a while.

When I went home from school, Mama asked, "What did you learn in school today?"

"We spent most of the time talking about the sinking of the *Lusitania*," I said. "We learned a lot."

"If you had a regular teacher, she would have stuck to the textbook," Mama said.

"We used our textbooks, Mama," I said. "Today, we had a real need for them."

Dad was resting on the couch. I thought he was asleep, but he must have been listening. "Why doesn't President Wilson do something about all that loss of American lives?" he asked.

"I'm glad he's a mild man," Mama said. "Teddy Roosevelt would have had us in the war by this time, and our boys would be dying in foreign lands. Helen's oldest boy, Colin, is already talking about enlisting in the National Guard."

"President Wilson is making a speech in Philadelphia to-night," Dad said. "Maybe it will be released early in the *Evening Bulletin*."

After supper, I went to the railroad station early so as to be sure to get a copy of the evening newspaper. It didn't have the president's speech. There was an article about international law and how it said that a warship could not destroy an enemy's merchant vessel without first stopping it, making sure of its nationality, and arranging for the safety of its passengers and crew. But the article also pointed out that this law had been made before the time of submarines, in the days of sailing ships, when an armed warship could easily stop a merchantman. Submarines were more vulnerable, and if one surfaced to warn a merchant vessel, the submarine might be destroyed if the ship was armed.

I took this clipping to school the next morning and read it to the geography class. By this time, most of us boys believed that President Wilson should ask Congress to declare war on Germany. The girls were divided. Dora suggested the British were trying to draw us into the war on their side. Her father, who was a lawyer, must have told her that.

The morning *Sun* carried President Wilson's speech in Philadelphia, and from what he said, it was plain he didn't want to lead us into the war. I clipped it. Here is one thing he said: "There is such a thing as a man being too proud to fight. There is such a thing as a nation being so right that it does not need to convince others by force that it is right."

Ric snorted when I read that in history class. "Suppose George Washington had believed that," he said. "We'd still be English colonies today. Sometimes, you've got to fight for your rights."

Teddy Roosevelt reacted about the same way Ric had. He

called President Wilson "Professor" Wilson, like he might have been an absent-minded college professor, and said he was supported by mollycoddles and pacifists.

When Ric clipped Roosevelt's speech and read it to our class, Dora read an article telling about the British blockade of Germany. It was aimed at defeating Germany by starving everyone.

"It's just as inhuman to starve people as to drown them," Dora said.

But as the days passed, the excitement that followed the sinking of the *Lusitania* subsided, and we began to study for our final examinations. Some of the girls told Miss Agnes it would have been better if we had stuck to our textbooks more and not argued so much about what the United States should have done after the sinking of the *Lusitania*.

5

🐚 *That Old Red Stutz*

It *was Saturday*—I went down to the river to shoot at water snakes. Ric came along carrying his air rifle; it was only a single-shooter.

"Say, Noah," he said, "let me try your pump gun." He gave me his so I handed mine over. Before I knew it, he had shot ten times at a bottle floating in the river.

"These repeaters ain't as powerful as my single shot," he said. "Let's go over to the dump and shoot rats."

Mama always tells me to keep away from the town dump. She can always smell me and tell when I've been there. She says it has all kinds of bad germs, but the hunting is good with big rats, and there's no telling what you can find if you poke around and have sharp eyes. You can't go barefoot because of the broken glass—outside of that and the smell it's a fine place. Anyway, me and Ric followed the creek and across the field to the dump pile.

You really need a rat terrier to flush the rats. We didn't see any. While we were hunting, a couple of wagons loaded with junk drove in and dumped it. As soon as they were gone, we started to poke around.

"Look what I found, Noah," Ric said, holding up a pint whiskey bottle. He pulled out the cork and sniffed.

"Boy, that must have been powerful stuff," he said. "Want a sniff?" I sniffed and Ric put the cork back in the bottle and stuck it in his hip pocket. The drugstore will give you two cents for an empty pint bottle.

Ric was luckier than me. In a couple of minutes, he found an empty tea kettle, only it had a hole in the bottom. Then my stick caught in something under some ashes, and it felt like a wheel. Wheels are a real find—I called Ric. We cleared the ashes away carefully and uncovered an old baby carriage with four good wheels. The axles were there, with a brake, and the wheels had rubber tires.

"I'll betcha the junk man will give me fifty cents for these wheels," I said, gloating over them.

"They belong to both of us," Ric said. "Didn't I let you sniff my whiskey bottle? We don't want to sell them to the junk man. Let's make an automobile."

"You let me smell your whiskey bottle, but then you put it in your pocket," I said.

"Aw, Noah, don't start to argue," Ric said. "I'll tell you what. I've got two wooden boxes we can use to make the body of the automobile, and I got the nails and paint, too."

I'd been wanting an automobile for some time. We don't have enough snow to use our sleds much. And Ric agreed to keep the wheels at my house while we were building the auto. Every day after school we worked on it. We fastened the axles to a piece of heavy oak with tenpenny nails, and used two tin cans for headlights, and the bottom of a peach basket for the steering wheel. Ric also brought a can of red paint that had enough to give our auto one good coat.

The paint wasn't even dry when we took a trial run down

Water Street. Ric rode down to the bridge and I pushed, then he pushed me home. She was fast and so quiet with those rubber tires.

"She runs just like that old red Stutz of Eddie Ricken-backer's," Ric said.

"I'll betcha she's the fastest one in town," I said.

"I don't know about that," Ric said. "Have you seen the one PeeWee Sumner got for Christmas?"

"It ain't got rubber tires," I said.

"No, but it's got ball bearings and you know what that means," Ric said. "Let's ride over to his house and take a look at it. Maybe he'll race us."

"He wouldn't race," I said. "His father wouldn't let him."

"Well, it ain't his fault that his father owns the basket factory and half the houses in town," Ric said. "Let's go over and look at his car anyway."

So we rode over to the big house where PeeWee lived. He was out on the sidewalk in front of his place with his new auto, playing by himself. He don't have much fun and is growing up to be a sissy.

"Good afternoon, PeeWee," Ric said, smart-like, "ain't you afraid of getting your clothes dirty playing outside of the house? Where's your nurse?"

The Sumner boy looked like he was going to cry. "I haven't had a nurse for several years," he said. "Don't you know any better than to say 'ain't?'" It's vulgar."

"You just said it," Ric replied, "so that makes you vulgar as well as being a sissy."

That poor little rich boy didn't have enough spunk to answer Ric or maybe he was too smart. He just looked at our old red Stutz.

"Where did you get that piece of junk you are pushing

around?" he said. He examined the wheels. "They're off a baby carriage. Ric and Noah riding around in a baby carriage."

But he didn't call us sissies; he knew better than to call us sissies.

"It certainly is a shame that you boys can't afford a real automobile like mine," he said. It was made of metal painted blue and had a real steering wheel with a horn that honked when you squeezed a rubber bulb.

"Looks ain't everything," Ric said. "Our old red Stutz is faster than yours—it has too much gingerbread on it. Our car is stripped for action."

PeeWee Sumner turned up his nose. "Talk is cheap," he said. "If I had a servant to push me, I'd show you how a real auto can travel." He examined our wheels again. "Baby carriage wheels on a soap box," he said, sneering.

Just then Crow Davis came along the street rolling a hoop. He stopped when he came to our autos—they were blocking the street.

"Well, PeeWee," Ric said, "here's your chance to back up your claims or shut up. Why don't you hire Crow to push you?"

The rich boy looked Crow over and acted like he might have wanted to feel his leg muscles, but he didn't. Crow is built well and a fast runner. Most of our colored folks are good at running—they have to be.

"Why not," PeeWee said, and jingled the coins in his pants pocket. "Boy, I'll pay you a quarter to push me and my auto in a mile race with that piece of junk with the wheels of a baby carriage."

"I'll do it if you give me the quarter first," Crow said. He didn't even seem to mind PeeWee calling him "Boy."

"O.K., Boy," PeeWee said, and he gave Crow the coin.

"Where we going to race to?" I asked.

"Let's run down to the foot of Water Street and up the hill past your house to Queen Street and follow it to Cannon Street and back to here," Ric said.

"That's all right with me," PeeWee Sumner said. "How about you riding, Ric, and letting Noah push you."

"You take care of your own car and we'll take care of our old red Stutz," Ric said. "Me and Noah are going to take turns riding and pushing. If you and Crow want to do that, it's all right with us."

We laughed, because we knew that no white boy would push a Negro, not even Crow Davis.

We lined up and Ric got into our car with me pushing. Off we went. Like I said, Crow is strong and fast; the blue auto pulled away from our red Stutz, and by the time it reached the foot of Water Street, PeeWee was fifty yards ahead of us. My tongue was hanging out, but Crow seemed as fresh as when we started. PeeWee kept looking back and waving. That made Ric mad. As we rounded the corner at the foot of the hill, Ric applied the brake and jumped out.

"Get in, Noah," he said. "I'll push."

Ric is bigger than I am and stronger. He dug in going up the hill and Crow must have been getting tired. By the time we turned the corner into Queen Street, we were only a few feet behind PeeWee. Then we passed them and gave them the dust for a change.

We were leaving them behind when I felt the steering wheel trembling and knew something was wrong. We stopped quickly and got out our tools. The front axle was loose, but we had a tenpenny nail to fix it with. While we were working on the axle, PeeWee and Crow passed us again, but Crow was panting badly and about ready to drop. He looked almost white.

I jumped into our car and Ric soon caught up with them in time to win the race by four lengths. Crow sank to the ground, exhausted, but PeeWee's face was as red as our car.

"Damn," he said. "Damn your baby carriage wheels," and he got out of his auto and kicked our red Stutz. That made him feel better, and you could see that even though he kicked it he saw our auto differently. He walked around it a couple of times and turned its steering wheel.

"I guess you know what a real fast car looks like now," Ric said, but he was looking at PeeWee's factory model when he said it.

"How about trading cars?" PeeWee asked.

Ric looked at me and I looked at Ric. We shook our heads meaning, "No."

"We won," Ric said, "we don't have no reason to trade."

PeeWee examined our car again and gave it a push. "It moves easily," he said, "even without ball bearings." Then he stuck his hand into his pocket and brought out two fifty-cent pieces.

"I'll give you an extra dollar with the trade," he said.

Ric looked at me and I looked at Ric. We took the coins.

PeeWee pushed our old red Stutz into his yard. He was smiling, and happy, at least for a while. Ric got into our shiny, new auto and I pushed him toward home, feeling like a millionaire with the fify-cent piece pressing against my leg. We could hear the ball bearings humming.

Mama saw us coming and met us at the gate. "Where did you get that?" she demanded.

"We just traded it for our car," I said.

"Traded?" she said. "Who traded you?"

"PeeWee Sumner."

"You mean that rich Sumner boy whose father owns half the town?" Mama asked.

"Yes, ma'am," I said.

"You take that auto right back to him and get yours," Mama said. "We ain't going to be beholden to the Sumners."

So we rode back to the big Sumner house and PeeWee was glad to see us coming. His father must have come home to lunch and seen our old red Stutz. We gave him his car and his money and took our auto. On the way home, I pushed Ric.

6

🐚 Spitting Nails

That *summer the crabs* were so late coming up the river that Dad took a job in the basket factory. I went to work with him. While we were eating breakfast that first day Mama warned me.

"Don't you put any nails in your mouth, Noah. You might swallow one."

"It wouldn't hurt him," Dad said. "The McClure boys swallow nails every day—it don't hurt them."

"The McClures are older than Noah and tougher," Mama said. "Noah already has a weak stomach without swallowing some of them sharp nails."

Joe and Jim McClure lived on our street and worked steady in the basket factory. They were the fastest basket makers in town and could make one every minute for an hour without stopping to rest. Their hammers hitting the nails sounded like the engine in Dad's bateau running at full speed—and their blows were just as regular. Before starting a basket, they put a handful of nails into their mouths; they pushed the nails out one at a time with their tongue. They had a phonograph and worked to music.

We were paid two cents for each peach basket. The McClure boys could make more than a dollar an hour for a ten-hour day. That was good money anywhere on the Eastern Shore in 1915. Watching the work, I could see something was driving them. When they stopped to smoke a cigarette or drink a bottle of sarsaparilla, they were nervous. It must have been hard to slow down after moving so fast for an hour.

The peach baskets were made on an iron form, a large wheel around which narrow strips of wood were stretched and nailed. Next the staves were nailed to the top strip with another strip on top of them. The circular form could be turned as you worked. With all the staves fastened to the top strip, a round wooden bottom was slipped on the other end of the form, and the staves were pulled down on it with an iron ring. Other strips were fastened over the bottoms of the staves and around the middle to finish the basket. Sometimes the factory also made bushel baskets and boxes, but that summer it was only manufacturing peach baskets.

Our first day at the basket factory was the hardest. We worked ten hours, with half an hour for lunch, and I only made twenty-five baskets. That amounted to fifty cents. One time Miss Louisa gave me fifty cents just for taking a letter to the train and mailing it.

Dad has made baskets before. He could spit nails, and while not anywhere as fast as the McClure boys, he made a hundred baskets for two dollars that first day. When we got home, Mama was putting supper on the table. "How did the work go?" she asked.

"I only made fifty cents," I said. "If you'd let me spit nails, I could make a lot more."

"Fifty cents is better than nothing," Mama said, and she held out her hand for the money we had made. "Don't hold anything back on me, George."

"I need a quarter for cigarettes," Dad said, giving her the rest.

"Tomorrow, we'll have meat cakes for supper," she said, "along with fresh lima beans and sugar corn from our garden."

Work increases your appetite. I ate more than usual, and then went up town to get a copy of the *Evening Bulletin*. But after a day in the basket factory, the war seemed farther away, and I went to bed without reading the newspaper.

The next day was easier. I worked next to Dad with Joe McClure on the other side of me. I was working faster, but before driving each nail, I had to pick it off the bench. That slowed me down.

Joe McClure was watching me out of the corner of his eye. "You're going to have to learn how to spit nails if you want to make any real money," he said, while he was smoking a cigarette after making fifty baskets.

"I promised Mama not to put any nails in my mouth," I said.

"Why don't you hold them between your lips?" Joe said. "That's the way I started. You couldn't swallow any that way."

Dad was listening and nodded his head—his mouth was full of nails.

That suited my conscience, and what Mama didn't know couldn't hurt her. I lined up ten small nails between my lips and began to make a basket. This helped a lot although Joe still made four baskets by the time I slipped the ring off the finished peach basket.

By the end of the day, I had made fifty baskets and took a dollar home. I didn't swallow any nails, but I had a bad taste in my mouth. Even the meat cakes that I especially liked didn't taste good. Mama noticed that I wasn't eating much.

"Don't you want another meat cake, Noah?" she asked.

"No, thanks," I said.

"You look pale," she said. "Did you eat anything else besides your lunch at the factory?"

"No, ma'am," I said, and asked to be excused from the table. I went out on the porch and sat in one of the rockers. Dad knew I wasn't feeling good, so he went up town and got the newspaper himself.

But I didn't have any trouble going to sleep, and when I awoke the next morning the bad taste was gone. It was Saturday. The basket factory only operated for half a day, and knowing this, the McClure boys really turned on the speed. They raced one another as their phonograph played "There'll Be a Hot Time in the Old Town Tonight." That music helped. I hammered in time to it or tried to. When Joe McClure stopped for sarsaparilla, he gave me a bottle.

"It'll take the taste of the nails out of your mouth," he said.

I didn't like the flavor of the sarsaparilla, but it was better than the nails. By the time the twelve o'clock whistle blew, I had made thirty baskets. Later, when I gave Mama the money, she returned it.

"You've been wanting to buy a new fishing pole and line for some time," she said.

That afternoon I bought a twelve-foot bamboo pole from the hardware store for a quarter. There was enough money left to buy a new line, two hooks with catgut, and a lead sinker, as well as an ice cream cone with two dips that I got at the drug store on the way to the river.

I searched the cove for a peeler crab without any luck and had to dig some worms. By the time I rigged the new line and reached my favorite piling on the old wooden bridge, it was three o'clock. The tide was right. I caught a fine string of white perch and a croaker that must have weighed two pounds. Mama fried the fish for supper.

After working in the basket factory only a few days, I could understand better why most folks in our town called Sunday "the day of rest." It would have been good to stay home the whole day, but Mama took me to church with her in the morning; I went to Sunday School that afternoon; and sang in the choir that night. I saw Ric in Sunday School.

"I'm working in the basket factory with Dad," I told him.

"Have you started to spit nails?" he asked.

"Mama won't let me," I explained.

"She holds pins in her mouth," Ric said. "It wouldn't hurt you to swallow one of those little nails you use making peach baskets. Suppose you were handling eightpenny nails like Pop does—that would be different."

I began to buy a couple of bottles of sarsaparilla at the grocery store on the way to the basket factory. It helped to take away the taste of the nails; by this time I was putting them into my mouth. But the taste of the soda pop lingered; it didn't help my appetite at mealtimes. On Saturday, when I weighed myself on the penny scale in front of the drugstore, the needle stopped at ninety-five pounds. At Easter, I had weighed 105 pounds, but some of this weight was my heavier clothing.

That second week I made seven dollars. That was as much as some of the clerks made in the stores, and they were grownup. But I was working for it—and also paying for it. On our way to the basket factory in the morning, me and Dad began to hurry along, our feet hit the pavement just like our hatchets hit the baskets ten hours a day. I was drinking three bottles of sarsaparilla a day. Dad didn't drink it, but he was smoking a pack of cigarettes a day and also rubbing snuff to take away the taste of the nails.

The McClure boys didn't seem to mind the nails or anything else. I was getting tired of hearing that same tune on their phonograph, over and over again, but they seemed to like it, or maybe they didn't really hear it anymore. They worked like two machines, rapidly and efficiently, not making any mistakes, and turning out a lot of baskets.

After work, they walked home along the same street we followed, but they soon left us behind, walking the same way they made baskets, faster and faster, looking straight ahead like walking was work, too. They were the best basket makers in town, but as Dad often says, everything has a price. They were paying for their success, even if they didn't know it.

I wasn't very successful as a basket maker, but I paid, too. One Sunday afternoon, after I had worked a month at the basket factory, I was ill after dinner and up-chucked everything. I didn't tell Mama, knowing how it would worry her, but that evening I had a chill and fever. She sent Dad to get Dr. Salmons.

He had me stick out my tongue and took my temperature. It was high. Then he wrote a prescription for calomel, and asked Mama what I was doing that summer. When she told him I was working at the basket factory, he said he didn't think that kind of piece-work was good for a young boy.

While I was sick, somebody told Mama I had been spitting nails. After I got better, she wouldn't let me go back to the basket factory. It was the middle of August, with only a couple of weeks before school, anyway.

7

She Did, Did She?

Mama was talking over the side fence to Mrs. Steers. "She ought to take care of her husband's sons. If she'll rear them right, we can mind our own sons."

"I guess she's not interested in them, being they're stepchildren," Mrs. Steers said. "That oldest boy might be her brother. I don't know how Mr. Eben could marry that young thing with Nellie hardly cold in the ground."

They were gossiping about Mr. Eben Pauley's new wife. Nobody knew he was planning to marry again until he went to the city on a business trip and came back married to a girl who was young enough to be his daughter. Now she had started a movement to turn the town dump into a children's playground.

"Noah doesn't need anybody to watch him play," Mama said. "There's plenty of pastures where the boys can play ball without turning the dump into a playground. It ain't like this was a big city with no place to play except the streets. We don't need no city woman to come down here and tell us how to raise our children."

"I like to play on the dump just as it is, Mama," I said. "Me and Ric find all kinds of things on the dump."

"There you are," Mama said. "Even a child knows it's foolishness."

"All of the men are supporting her," Mrs. Steers said. "My husband thinks her ideas are wonderful."

"You know how men are," Mama said, looking to see if I was listening. "My daughter, Helen, told me she pulls her dress up over her knees when she gets into Mr. Eben's automobile. You know what uplift the men are interested in."

"I'm going to have to talk to Mr. Steers," Mrs. Steers said.

"George never had any nerve with women," Mama said. "Everything has its advantages."

I remembered being with Dad when he had given Mrs. Pauley a trout less than a week ago. She and Mr. Eben live in a big house across the cove from us. She had wandered down to the river while Dad was working on the engine of his bateau. He had the top of the cylinder off and was cutting out a new gasket. It was so powerful that it blew out a gasket almost every month.

"Good morning," Mrs. Pauley said. "My, how do you fix that motor? It looks very complicated."

"Yes, ma'am," Dad said, and went on cutting out the gasket with his penknife.

"Did you catch that big fish?" Mrs. Pauley said, pointing to the trout lying in the bottom of the boat.

"I caught it, then blew out the gasket coming home."

"Oh," Mrs. Pauley said. "Would you sell it to me? Mr. Pauley was saying this morning that he would like to have some fried fish for supper." When she smiled it did something to you.

Dad looked up and was caught in her smile. "You can have it if you want it," he said. "It ain't a very choice trout but you're welcome to it." He reached in the boat and picked it up.

"Oh, thank you," Mrs. Pauley said. "Do I cook it just like it is, head and all?"

Dad looked at her but she seemed serious. "No, ma'am, it has to be cleaned."

"Oh," Mrs. Pauley said, looking helpless.

"I'll clean it for you," Dad said, and laying down the new gasket he got the trout ready for the frying pan. Mrs. Pauley turned her head the other way when he slit the trout's belly and pulled out its intestines. She saw me for the first time.

"Is this your little boy?" she asked.

"Yes, ma'am," Dad said, "that's Noah."

"Hello, Noah," she said. "Are you helping your father?"

"No ma'am, I'm just playing."

"Playing?" she asked, looking around her. "How can you play by yourself without proper equipment or a supervisor?"

"I've been skipping oyster shells," I said, picking up one and sailing it across the cove. It skipped five times.

"That must be fun," she said, watching the shell skip. "Aren't you afraid you will hit someone or break a window?"

"Not when you know how to throw them," I said.

She seemed interested. "Show me how to throw one, Noah."

I found one that would sail a long way with half a chance and showed her how to hold it. Her fingernails were long and painted red.

"I used to play basketball in college," she said, and tossed a beauty, a real long one, but it went the wrong way. It sailed all the way across the cove and right through one of Mrs. Pauley's windows.

She looked at me and burst out laughing. Somehow, I couldn't help laughing. We all laughed, even Dad.

"I'll be seeing you," she said and walked away carrying the trout by its tail.

Almost everybody in town was talking about Mr. Eben's new wife. Before school started the other day, Miss Laura was in our room talking with Miss Gussie.

"They say the mayor has promised her he will change the dump into a playground if she will raise a thousand dollars," Miss Laura said.

"I heard she is planning to put on a show with local talent," Miss Gussie said. "That means more work for us. We'll do the work and she'll get the credit."

Even Ric was interested in Mrs. Pauley when I met him in the washroom. "Noah, did you hear about that city woman planning to ruin our dump?" he asked.

"You mean Mrs. Pauley?" I asked.

"I don't know what her name is," Ric said, "but I don't want to play on no playground. I like to play in the pastures with the dump to hunt rats and for foraging."

"If we did have a playground, Miss Lizzie couldn't keep the balls we knock over her fence," I said. "I betcha we'd have better baseballs, too."

"That woman has got you, too," Ric said, looking disgusted.

I didn't tell him how I had showed her how to throw an oyster shell.

"Nobody is going to tell me where or how to play," Ric said. "It's bad enough to be told how to work."

"We'd better go back to class," I said. It was awfully embarrassing to have Miss Gussie rap on the boys' washroom door and call out your name.

It turned out that the teachers' gossip was correct. There was going to be a show, and since the money was going to be used for a children's playground, we would be the ones who gave it. Mrs. Pauley never thought of asking us if we wanted a playground. I sort of held that against her, even though she laughed when she threw an oyster shell through her own window.

The teachers were asked to pick the best actors and actresses from each grade. Miss Gussie read her list on Friday afternoon, just before dismissal. My name was on it. So was Ric's.

"I won't do it," Ric said. "I'll run away from home before I make a monkey of myself on that stage. What are you going to do, Noah?"

"I don't know," I said. "It gives me goose pimples just to think about it."

When I got home, I was still worried and Mama sensed that something was wrong.

"You didn't have any trouble in school today, did you Noah?" she asked.

"No ma'am," I said, "except Miss Gussie has picked me to act in Mrs. Pauley's play."

"She did, did she?" Mama said.

"Do I have to act in it if I don't want to, Mama?"

"We'll see," she said, "but you ought to be proud that Miss Gussie chose you. Who else did she choose?"

"She picked Ric. He says he'll run away from home before he'll act like a monkey."

"Don't you listen to that Ricard," Mama said. "You wouldn't run away from home, would you?"

"No, ma'am," I said.

Dad had been listening.

"Is that the show Mrs. Pauley is organizing to raise money for the playground?" he asked.

"Yes, sir," I said.

Mama dropped the potato she was peeling. "That woman ought to stay home and take care of her husband's children. Mrs. Steers told me yesterday that they sent Mr. Eben's oldest boy off to a military academy last week. When they won't take care of them at home, they send them away to a military school."

"It'll be nice to have that old dump changed into a pretty

playground with benches in the shade to rest on," Dad said.

"Your playing days are over, George," Mama said.

"You ought to be proud to have Noah act in the show," Dad said.

"Maybe I ought to, but I hate to see him helping that city woman," Mama said.

"Have you ever seen her or talked to her?" Dad asked.

"No, and I don't want to," Mama said, starting to get jealous. "Have you?"

"She came down to the river one day while I was working on the bateau," Dad said.

"She did, did she," Mama said. "At your age, I don't want to see you making a fool of yourself."

"Nothing happened, Mother," Dad said. "Noah was with me."

Mama looked at me.

"Nothing happened," I said. "Dad gave Mrs. Pauley a trout and she threw an oyster shell that sailed right through one of her windows."

When I mentioned the fish, Dad left the couch and slipped out the back door.

"Do I have to act in Mrs. Pauley's play, Mama?" I asked.

"We'll see what the other mothers do," she said.

Mama and the other parents did a lot of talking that next week. Every day was like Sunday, with Mama putting on her black silk dress and rustling away after supper to call on other parents. But most of them thought it was a good idea to have a playground with a supervisor to take care of their children. So Mama gave in.

"Since the other children are going to act in the show, so should you, Noah," she said. "I'm proud that Miss Gussie chose you."

When the teachers started to work on the show, it turned out to be not a play but something like vaudeville, with singing, dancing, recitations, and even a debate. Mrs. Pauley decided that the boys in Miss Gussie's class would give the debate. I was in it and so was Ric. He seemed to like the idea and didn't say anything more about running away.

"I'm going to speak just like Senator Burton does on the Fourth of July," he said. "I'll pause to drink some water and gargle to rest my throat."

Miss Gussie helped us organize our arguments. The subject was, "Resolved: That the pen is mightier than the sword." The night before the show, Mrs. Pauley had what she called a full dress rehearsal, when we put all of the parts of the show together and wore the costumes that we would have in the show. Mrs. Pauley sat in a chair close to the stage and told us how to improve it.

"That song is much too slow," she said when Dora was singing "Beautiful Ohio." "Just because it is a waltz, you don't have to drag it."

Mrs. Pauley didn't like the dancing, either. "You two move across the stage like a pair of sick cows," she said to the couple who were dancing in wooden shoes.

She was bored almost to death with our debate. After we had finished, she sighed. "It reminds me of a filibuster in the U.S. Senate, boys," she said, and suggested that we wear roses in our lapels on the night we had the debate.

The ticket sale was a great success, with every seat sold out and standing room only on the night of the show. Even Dad was going and about the only time he went to a show was to see the minstrels. The program started out with the little kids and they made plenty of mistakes, but it was cute when they said the wrong things or came on the stage at the wrong time. Everybody laughed and applauded.

Our debate was the last thing on the program. We were all wearing big white roses like Mrs. Pauley had suggested. Ric had a long cigar wrapped in tinsel paper sticking out of his breast pocket where everybody could see it. He was the first speaker, and in spite of flashing the big cigar, he was scared half to death. His knees shook and he leaned on the rostrum for support. After addressing the chairman and sneering at his opponents, he coughed and had to pour himself a glass of water from the pitcher. That steadied him.

I'd heard him practice his speech in the woodshed; it was good and started like this: "In this great country of ours with its more than three million square miles," then he would pause to let the figures sink in.

Now he put his arm on the rostrum for support and braced himself. "Friends," he said, "in this great country with its more than three million square heads," and he paused to let it sink in. When Ric mentioned the three million square heads, the audience gasped before howling with laughter and clapping. They must have thought it was a part of the show. Ric looked like he might sink right through the stage, then he laughed, too, and I could see that he wasn't scared anymore. From then on, he had the audience with him.

I was the last speaker in the debate. It's better to be first and get it over with—then you can relax and watch the others suffer. I sat there, holding the sheets of paper on which I had written what I was going to say tightly in my hands. Those papers were the only thing that held me together. I knew that I could read what was on them, even if my voice trembled. It wasn't necessary to remember what to say, like with a play or recitation.

It was a warm evening in April, and the windows of the auditorium were all open. The proprietor of the furniture store had placed one of the new electric fans near the stage. It was a large one and kept us cool, but the hum of the fan made it necessary for us to speak louder. I sat there waiting, listening to the speakers and the hum of the fan, and to a regular knocking sound that I suddenly realized was my heart. When I recognized the source of the beating, my heart began to race and skip beats as it does when I'm excited.

Erny Salmons started to speak; I followed him. I looked over my papers, making sure that they were arranged in their proper order. Erny finished and sat down, grinning, happy to be through, and I approached the rostrum. We had borrowed it from the Methodist church for the occasion. I addressed the chairman, the honorable judges, my worthy opponents—said with a sneer—fond teachers, loving parents, and others before placing my papers on the rostrum. When my legs started to tremble, I leaned on the rostrum, cleared my throat, and began to speak, or rather, read from my speech. After the first few lines, my voice became stronger and I looked out at the audience. They appeared to be listening. I began to relax.

When I came to the end of my first argument, I hit the rostrum with my fist to emphasize the point, just as Miss Gussie had taught us.

This was a mistake. The wind from my fist blew the papers off the rostrum and they were caught in the current caused by the electric fan. My papers sailed away like the paper airplanes we made, and several disappeared through the open window.

Without my papers I was lost and stood gripping the rostrum, silent, staring out of the window. I thought of following the papers, but some of the audience must have realized my plight and helped to recover them. Somehow I completed my arguments, and reached a point where I knew that I would finish—after that I got stronger and must have convinced someone. Anyway, the judges declared us the winners.

I didn't see Mama and Dad after the show and went home by myself. Later they came home bringing some ice cream with them.

"I guess everybody will laugh at me tomorrow," I said.

"Fiddlesticks," Mama said. "They've got someone bigger to laugh at."

"Did you notice Mrs. Pauley wasn't there tonight?" Dad asked.

"Why wasn't she?" I asked.

"She's run off with Mr. Pauley's bank clerk," Mama said, "the young one with the curly hair. They just got into Mr. Eben's new automobile and drove away."

8

🌿 *Sweeter than Violets*

It *was only four weeks* before the county track meet. Miss Gussie was taking entries for our grade.

"We need four boys to run the 440-yard relay in the ninety-five-pound class," she said.

That was the race we had won in the eighty-pound class, last year, Erny, Mickey, Ric, and me. We all held up our hands.

"That's the race for us, Miss Gussie," I said, and she took our names. "Are you sure you boys are not too heavy?" she asked. "You've been gaining weight all winter, Noah. Are you sure you're not too heavy?"

After school the four of us met in the boys' room. "We'll have to start training for the relay as soon as it gets a little warmer," Mickey said.

"Let's wait until we take off our long underwear," Erny said. "When you run, it makes you itchy."

That was the middle of March. April Fools' Day came and we fooled everybody but Miss Gussie. That afternoon just before dismissal she rang the bell on her desk.

"I want all of the boys to stay after school today," she said. "I have something important to tell you."

We all began to wonder what she had found out. "Do you reckon it's about the writing and pictures in the boys' room?" Ric asked.

"She never goes in there," Mickey said.

"Maybe they're trying to find out who broke the window in the hall," Erny said. He had a guilty look.

When the dismissal bell rang, the girls all marched out, making faces at us boys. Miss Gussie sat at her desk, and took out a set of papers to mark, but she didn't even notice us. We sat and waited—until Ric couldn't stand it any longer and held up his hand.

"Yes, Ricard," Miss Gussie said.

"You had something important to tell us, Miss Gussie," he said.

"Yes, Ricard," but she didn't tell us, and went back to marking the papers.

We sat quietly for what seemed like an hour waiting for Miss Gussie, until I raised my hand and rattled the desk to get her attention.

"What is it that you are going to tell us, Miss Gussie?" I asked.

She smiled, only it was almost a grin. "April Fool, boys," she said, "April Fool to all of you, and now you may go home."

In the boys' room, we all agreed it would be better not to tell the others why Miss Gussie kept us in.

After that the days started to get warmer. One morning on the way to school, I picked a bunch of violets for Miss Gussie because she was my favorite teacher, only I put them in my pocket so that the other boys couldn't see them. I was early, the first one in our room except Miss Gussie. Nobody ever gets to school before her. I took the violets out of my pocket and straightened them.

"Here's some violets for you, Miss Gussie," I said.

She blushed like a girl. "You picked them for me, Noah?"

"Yes, ma'am," I said, "only please don't tell the other kids where you got them or they'll tease me."

"I won't tell a soul," she said, and got a vase out of the book closet. I filled it with water and she placed the violets on her desk.

Every once in a while all morning, Miss Gussie would look at the violets. They were pretty, after the cold winter. Even teachers must be glad when the spring comes and flowers bloom. That same day we began training for the relay.

"We'd do better if we had a coach," Ric said.

"What does a woman know about running?" Erny asked. "They would just slow us down."

"I wasn't thinking of a woman," Ric said. "Maybe we could get Mr. Blake to coach us." He's the manual arts teacher in the high school, but we're all in the same building.

"I never thought of him," Erny said. "Do you think he knows anything about running?"

"He sure does," Ric said. "When Miss Gussie sent me to Mr. Manning's office last week, we were talking, and he told me that Mr. Blake once held the state record for the hundred yard dash. He was that fast."

"You'd never know it today," Erny said.

"That's just because he's a school teacher," I said. "Did you ever see a man teacher who wasn't like a preacher, the way they talk and walk?"

"That must be it," Ric said. "I'd never want to be a teacher, not even a manual arts teacher."

"Let's go down to the shop and ask him," I said.

"Do you think Miss Gussie would let us?" Erny asked.

"If Noah asks her she will," Ric said. "Noah's her pet."

"Go on and ask her, Noah," Erny said.

"Aw, I don't want to," I said.

"You must be scared," Mickey said.

"All right," I said, not wanting to be called that, and raised my hand.

"Yes, Noah," Miss Gussie said, smiling.

"Could us boys who run in the relay go down and speak to Mr. Blake?" I asked.

"You want to speak to Mr. Blake?" she asked, not knowing what it was about.

"Yes, ma'am," I said. "We want to ask him if he will coach our relay team."

"Oh, is that what you want to see him about?" she said. "He's teaching a class now."

"We won't bother him if he's busy," Mickey said.

"Can't we ask him, Miss Gussie?" Erny chimed in. "We want to win the relay. Mr. Blake used to be a champion runner."

Miss Gussie flushed. It's funny, but teachers never like you to say anything good about another teacher. "Whoever told you that?" she demanded, like Erny didn't know what he was talking about.

"Mr. Manning told me," Ric said. "Mr. Blake held the state record for the hundred-yard dash when he was in college."

"You'd never know he'd ever been that fast," Miss Gussie said.

"May we go see him?" Mickey begged.

"All right," Miss Gussie said, "but be sure you don't go anywhere else. I'll expect you back in five minutes."

"Yes, ma'am," we all said and tiptoed toward the door. When Alvin stuck out his foot to trip me, I stepped on it like I didn't see it.

"Ow," he yelled, and he wasn't pretending.

"What's the matter with you, Alvin?" Miss Gussie asked.

"Noah stepped on my foot," he said.

"Is that so, Noah?"

"I stepped on something," I said. "It was sticking out in the middle of the aisle and almost tripped me."

"Hereafter keep your feet under your desk, Alvin," Miss Gussie ordered.

There is something so wonderful about getting out of the classroom when the others are still inside, even if it's only for five minutes. We were quiet in the hall, but peeped into several classrooms on our way. Erny started Miss Laura's class laughing by thumbing his nose in front of the glass panel in the door. She got a glimpse of him and ran toward the door, but we were down the stairs before she could see us. When I rapped on Mr. Blake's door, he couldn't hear us, there was so much hammering and sawing inside. I'll be glad when I'm in the seventh grade and can make a stool with a leather cushion.

"Let's go in," Ric said, and opened the door. The rest of us followed him inside.

Mr. Blake was fastening a chair together with glue and clamps. "Hello, boys," he said. "What's wrong? Is Miss Gussie's door stuck again?"

"No, sir," Ric said. "We came to ask a favor of you."

"If it's something you want me to make in the shop, forget it," Mr. Blake said. "Outside of the desks and blackboards, I practically furnished this school since I came here."

"It's nothing like that," Ric said. "We wanted you to coach our relay team."

"Where'd you ever get the idea that I could coach you?" Mr. Blake asked, and I could see that he was pleased.

"Mr. Manning told me that you used to hold the state record for the hundred-yard dash," Ric said.

"I thought everybody had forgotten about that," Mr. Blake said. "What relay are you entered in?"

"The 440-yard relay for the ninety-five-pound class," Mickey said.

"I'm awfully busy," Mr. Blake said. "Right now we are making the scenery for the senior play."

"If you could tell us what to do and watch us once in a while, that would be enough," Ric said. "With your help, we might set a new state record."

"You might," Mr. Blake said. "Suppose that I meet you on the playground after school tomorrow."

"Yes, sir," we all said and ran all the way back to Miss Gussie's room. It had warmed enough for us to take off our long underwear and it was easier to run. After school I ran all the way home.

"What are you panting about, Noah?" Mama demanded. "You don't have a touch of spring grippe, do you?" She put her hand on my forehead. "You are warm."

"It's from running all the way home," I said. "We're training for the relay in the county track meet."

"That again," she said. "I don't know why they don't let you grow up naturally. They're always planning this or that. Last fall it was a show and now you're planning to run around a track like a race horse."

"Yes, ma'am," I said.

"Since you are in a running mood, suppose you gallop up to the store for me," she said, and made out the order and gave me the money. I ran up to Mr. Leary's store and all the way home, not Scout's pace but sprinting. Ric met me uptown and ran home with me.

"We ought to pin numbers on our backs," Ric said, "then people would know why we are running."

"You're right," I said. "The way we are running, people might think there is a fire somewhere."

"Frank Merriwell always ran along the country roads when he was training for a race," Ric said.

"It's good to lay off smoking," I said. "Even cornsilk might cut our wind."

"Maybe Mr. Blake will give us a talk on training," Ric said. "I can hardly wait until tomorrow."

The next day, we relay runners were mighty good in school so Miss Gussie wouldn't keep us in. She's fair enough, but it wouldn't hurt her conscience to keep us from seeing Mr. Blake. I don't know why teachers are so jealous. I had to be careful not to tangle with Ric. When he hit me with a spitball soaked in ink, I didn't do anything. Later at recess time, I did get a mouthful of water and wet him. After that, he let me alone and deviled Dora, so I guess he must have decided that we were even. Anyway, none of us four runners had to stay in, and when the dismissal bell rang, we ran out to the playground. Mr. Blake wasn't there but he showed up in a couple of minutes.

"Hello, boys," he said. "Where are your running togs?"

We hadn't thought of that. We wore our bathing suits the day of the meet, but we practiced beforehand in our regular clothes.

"Can't we run like we are?" Mickey asked.

"You can, but if you dress lighter with running shoes, it will cut your time. You should wear a pair of shorts and a sleeveless jersey. Since the track is not cinders, sneakers will be all right instead of spiked shoes."

We agreed to be uniformed the next time he saw us.

"Which one of you is the fastest?" our coach asked.

"Last year, Noah was," Mickey said.

"We'll see," our coach said. "All of you go over to the other side of the playground and I'll start you." He marked a line in the dirt with a stick. "Let's see who will be the first to cross this line."

We ran over to the edge of the playground and waited. "Get on your mark," Mr. Blake called. We crouched over in a line. "Get set! Go!"

Mickey got the start on the rest of us, but I passed him and was five yards ahead at the finish line.

"It looks like Noah is the fastest," our coach said. "That means he will run last. Who was leading at the start?"

"I was," Mickey said.

"Then you will run first," coach said. "Ric will be second and Erny third. Have you boys started training yet?"

"Yes, sir," Ric said. "We have been running a lot."

"That helps to build your strength and wind," coach said. "You should run on a track. I'll ask Coach Lewis at the college if we can run on their track. In the meantime, you boys get your togs. Let's plan to practice again in a couple of days."

I ran all the way home.

"You're panting like a race horse," Mama said.

"Mr. Blake is coaching us," I replied, "and he says we should have running togs."

"Now it's running togs," Mama said. "I don't know what the world is coming to. Last week I made a pair of walking bloomers for the wife of one of the college professors."

"Yes, ma'am," I said.

"I'll make them for you," she said, "but why do you need bloomers to take a walk?"

"If you make me running togs, it will save my school clothes," I said.

"I hadn't thought of that," she said. "All that running and sweating is hard on them."

"All I need is a pair of trunks and a jersey."

"I'll cut off a pair of your old pants for the trunks," she said, "but mind you, as soon as you stop running, put on your long pants again so you won't catch cold."

"Yes, ma'am," I said, wondering where I would get an athletic jersey.

A couple of days later, Mr. Blake took us up to the college on the hill. "You boys can dress in the locker room," he said.

It was great to be in the locker room and made us feel like real athletes—that smell of the locker room was sweeeter than violets. A lot of jerseys were hanging up with numbers on them. I had a pair of trunks and no jersey.

Coach Lewis must have heard us talking and came in from his office. "Where are you kids from?" he asked, looking stern. He was short and getting bald, but you could tell he was a good coach. His blue eyes could look right through you.

"Mr. Blake brought us from the school to use your track," Mickey said.

"So you're the relay team he called about," the college coach said, looking at me. "You're not going to run in your shirt are you?"

"That's all I got," I said.

"Just a minute," he said and left. When he returned he was carrying a sleeveless jersey. It was made in the college's colors, maroon and black, with the number thirteen on its back. "Here's a jersey that has shrunk so badly that no one can use it," he said. "You can have it."

"Thank you, sir," I said, and as I slipped the jersey on, all the other fellows were looking at me. We ran out to the athletic field like the college football team runs onto the gridiron, but the band wasn't playing and the bleachers were empty, except for Mr. Blake. He had a stopwatch and a pistol.

"Ain't you superstitious about that number thirteen, Noah?" Erny said. "How about trading jerseys?"

"I'm not superstitious about numbers," I said.

"I'll give you my penknife to boot," he said.

"I'm not swapping this jersey, ever," I said.

"All right, boys," Mr. Blake called, "separate around the track. You stay here, Mickey."

"We don't have a stick to carry, Coach," Erny said.

"Look around for one," he said, "later on I'll get you a bamboo baton."

While we were searching for a stick, a couple of the college boys came along. They were wearing skull caps and smoking big pipes with curved stems.

"Where did you get that college jersey, boy?" one of them asked me.

"Coach Lewis gave it to me," I said.

"Do you know who used to wear that jersey?" the other college boy asked me.

"No, sir," I said.

"That belonged to the great 'Guts' Gordy. He was wearing it when he set a new record for the mile run. It still stands after fifteen years."

"Jerusalem!" Mickey said, "think of it, wearing the same jersey that belonged to 'Guts' Gordy."

"See that you are worthy of the jersey, boy," the college fellow said.

"I'll try, sir," I said, and ran off to take my position at the three-quarter mark. Erny had the farthest to go, on the opposite side of the track. When we were all in our places, Mr. Blake pointed the pistol over his head and I saw a puff of smoke. Mickey raced around the long curve and handed the baton to Ric. It seemed that he took a long time to reach Erny, but I had it a few seconds later and carried it back to Coach Blake.

He looked at his stopwatch. "It took you boys sixty-three seconds," he said. "That's slow. You probably wasted five seconds passing the baton. Let's practice that now."

He showed us how to pass the baton without slowing your pace. "Let's run it again and see if you can cut your time to less than a minute," he said. We did—it was fifty-eight seconds that time.

"That'll be enough for today," Coach Blake said. "You fellows take a shower and dress."

It was like that for the next two weeks. Our best time was fifty-five seconds. Three days before the county track meet, we had finished our workout when Mr. Blake came into the locker room.

"Let's check your weights, boys," he said, "just to be certain that all of you are in the ninety-five-pound class."

There was a scale in Coach Lewis's office. "Step on, Mickey, you're our first runner," our coach ordered. He tipped the scales at ninety pounds. "O.K.," Mr. Blake said. Ric and Erny were all right, too.

But when I stepped on the scales it stopped at ninety-eight pounds. I had a heavy feeling in my stomach, too.

"You're three pounds overweight, Noah," our coach said.

"Maybe the scales are wrong," Ric said.

"There's nothing wrong with these scales," Coach Lewis said; he had been watching us weigh in. "If that lad wants to run in the relay, he'll have to lose three pounds."

"How will I do that?" I asked, all confused.

"You'll have to sweat it off," the college coach said. "Put on a couple of suits of long, heavy underwear, and a couple of sweaters over your clothing, and run it off."

"We'll run with you, Noah," Ric said.

"Cut down on your eating and don't drink much water," Coach Lewis added.

"We'll be around to your house after supper tonight, Noah," Ric said. "Be ready to take a long run in the country."

We would have beef stew for supper; it's one of my favorites. Dad likes it, too.

"Fill up your plate, again, Noah," he said. "This stew will really put the weight on you."

"I'm training for the race Friday, Dad," I said. "I don't think I should eat any more."

"Here I spend most of the afternoon making beef stew and you hardly touch it," Mama complained.

"I'll eat more next week, Mama," I said.

After supper I went upstairs and got my long underwear out of the bureau drawer. I had just finished putting on two suits when Mama came upstairs and saw me.

"What are you doing?" she demanded. "As hot as it's getting and you are putting on your long underwear again." She examined me closely. "You've got two suits of your long underwear on. Are you going crazy?"

"No, ma'am," I said. "I just want to sweat and lose three pounds."

"That sounds crazy to me," Mama said. "I thought you wanted to grow and put on weight."

"I do, Mama," I said, "but now I've got to lose three pounds so I can be in the ninety-five-pound class for the relay on Friday."

"Why didn't you say so in the first place?" she said.

Somebody knocked on the front door and I heard Dad talking to them. "Noah," he called, "there are three boys here to see you."

"I'll be right down," I called back and picked up a couple

of sweaters before Mama could change her mind and stop me.

The other fellows were dressed in their running togs. "Let's run across the bridge toward Church Hill," Ric said.

I could hardly run with all the clothing, so we stopped at Klinefeller's Woods to rest. Then we ran toward home.

"If we go down to the railroad station, you can weigh yourself on the penny scale," Mickey suggested. So we ran uptown, but when we got to the station, none of us had a penny.

Rip Parr came along and gave us one. I weighed ninety-nine pounds. "Something is wrong," I said.

"It's all the clothes you're wearing," Ric said. "Take them off."

"I can't undress here," I said. "A train might come along loaded with people."

"You know a train ain't due until seven," Mickey said. "I'd take them off if I was you."

"You're not me," I said. "I'm going home, anyway."

Mama was waiting for me. "Look at you, you poor, little wilted thing, and wringing wet," she said. Mama makes me sick when she talks like that.

"Aw, stop it," I said.

"How many pounds did you lose?" she asked.

"According to the scales, I gained a pound."

It was like that until the day of the meet as I tried all of the scales in town. One day I was down to ninety-three pounds, but the next day I weighed ninety-nine pounds again. Mr. Blake got worried and found another boy, Norris Rouse, to run in my place in case I was still too heavy. Norris is a nice boy, and he is a fast runner when some other boy is chasing him; nobody can catch him when he's scared, but we didn't know how fast he could run in the relay.

The night before the race, I was sitting with Dad on the porch while Mama was washing the dishes. "You didn't eat much supper tonight, Noah," he said. "Are you still overweight?"

"I'm not certain, Dad," I said.

"When do you get weighed?" he asked.

"Anytime after nine o'clock tomorrow morning. The relay isn't run until one thirty."

Dad rocked for a while. "The thing for you to do is not to eat any breakfast, or drink anything until you are weighed in the morning," he said. "After that you can eat a big lunch to make up for it."

"That's a good idea, Dad," I said. "I'll do it that way."

In the morning, I dressed in my running togs and ran all the way to the athletic field at the college where they were having the meet. Just as I suspected, they were using the same scales that were in Coach Lewis's office. I took off my sneakers before stepping on the scales. The bar teetered around ninety-five pounds.

"That's awfully close," the weigher said uncertainly.

"May I take off my jersey?" I asked.

"All right," he said, and pulling the maroon and black jersey over my head, I dropped it.

"You just made it, sonny," the official said, and stamped "95 lb. class" on my wrist.

I saw Ric down at the end of the line and showed him my stamp.

"Old No. 13 wasn't unlucky anyway," he said.

I went home and ate a big breakfast, or maybe it was an early lunch. On the way I had to stop and suck some early honey-suckle—I was that weak. But after Mama fed me flapjacks and eggs, I was ready for anything.

After the excitement of getting weighed, the race didn't seem very important. We won easily and set a new county record.

That sort of swelled our heads until Mr. Blake took us to Baltimore for the state meet. We didn't even place there. The track was made of cinders and all the other runners wore spiked shoes. They were faster, too.

9

🐚 We All Screamed

"**W**e've *been going* to Tolchester in the hacks from the livery stable as long as I can remember and we've never had an accident," Mama said. "It's just like our young rector to decide to ride in those newfangled automobiles. The young don't mind taking chances with their own lives or other people's."

She was talking about our new rector, Reverend Francis X. Hammond; he was only twenty-four, and ours was his first parish. Always in late August, our Sunday School went on a picnic to Tolchester, an amusement park located on Chesapeake Bay, twelve miles from our town. During the summer, excursion steamboats, the *Louise*, the *Emma Giles*, and others carried large crowds of Baltimoreans across the bay for a day at Tolchester. But in late August the steamers were not crowded and did not run every day—that was when we had our Sunday School picnic. And this year, our rector had decided to use automobiles, some owned by parishioners and others hired for the occasion, instead of the horse-drawn hacks from Greenley's Livery Stable.

"Horses are a lot safer than these gasoline buggies," Mama said. "Anybody with gumption knows that."

"How about the time the horses drawing our hack ran away

going down the hill to Tolchester?" Dad said. "It was almost as scary as riding on the Whirlpool Dip."

"You would remember that," Mama said. "Nobody was hurt. That reminds me of another thing—Noah, you are not to go on that Whirlpool Dip. Riding on the roller coaster is like taking off in a flying machine, only you got wheels instead of wings. Someday somebody is going to get killed—then they will close it down."

Kids under twelve weren't allowed to ride on the Whirlpool Dip, it was that terrifying. Now that I was thirteen and could ride on the roller coaster, Mama wouldn't let me. I didn't feel too bad about her decision; just to watch those little cars speeding around the curves and up and down the hills, while the riders were screaming, was enough for me. I've always had a big imagination.

A couple of days before the Sunday School picnic, I met Ric uptown.

"How much money have you saved for the picnic, Noah?" he asked.

"I've got a couple of dollars," I said. "Dad usually gives me a couple more."

"I've got almost five dollars," Ric said. "This year I'm going to win one of those horse pistols they award as prizes at the shooting gallery. Now we are old enough, let's go on the Whirlpool Dip. We'll get some girls to go with us and scare them half to death."

"Mama won't let me go on the roller coaster," I said.

"You're just making that up, Noah," Ric said. "You're scared to go."

"I'd rather win a Kewpie Doll on the gambling wheel," I said.

"Those gambling wheels are fixed," Ric said. "You don't have a chance. Besides, who wants to be carrying a doll baby around?"

"I'm going to give the one I win to Dora," I said.

Ric didn't like that. He figured Dora was his girl ever since they had started to hide together when we played Hide and Seek after choir practice.

"Dora would rather ride with me on the roller coaster," he said. "If she screams, I'll put my arm around her."

"You can't even get her to go on the Whirlpool Dip," I said.

"You wait and see," Ric said. "If anybody backs down, it will be you."

That was on Wednesday. Mama spent the next couple of days getting ready for the picnic. That afternoon she baked a three-layer cake with chocolate icing. On Thursday morning, I beat the dough to make the biscuits she baked with a chicken. She made lots of deviled eggs and sent me to the grocery store to buy a bottle of stuffed olives. They were special.

Friday morning, Dad gave me a couple of dollars before Mama and I left for the church.

"There's plenty of food in the refrigerator, George," she said. "The Lord willing, we'll be back in time to get your supper."

At the church we were assigned to different automobiles. Mama insisted that I go with her, along with Ric and his mother. You might have thought it was the first time Mama had ever ridden in an auto.

"I can't get out of this machine soon enough," she said as we rolled out of town and into the open country. The road had a hard surface. We moved along at a speed faster than most of us had ever traveled before. We must have been going more than thirty miles an hour, but the Model-T Ford we were riding in didn't have a speedometer. We could only guess our speed.

"You want to slow down before you get to that hill coming into Tolchester," Mama warned the driver, "or we'll all end up in the Chesapeake Bay."

"I've just had the auto's brakes tightened," the driver said, and stepped on the brake pedal to show Mama how quickly he could slow down and stop the auto. When the brakes squealed, Mama grabbed her hat.

"We might as well be riding on the Whirlpool Dip," she said, and closed her eyes when we came to a hill.

My own stomach was turning over. Only Ric seemed to be enjoying the ride. "Someday, I'm going to drive my own automobile across the country to California," he said.

The lane that connected the main road to Tolchester was a dirt one and during the summer it was very dusty. When we had traveled in the horse-drawn hacks, by the time we got to Tolchester we were covered with dust. The autos also stirred the dust, but our driver kept a good distance behind the car in front of us. Even Mama had to admit that the ride in the automobile was cleaner and faster.

"I've never traveled so fast in my life," she said as she climbed out of the car, carrying the chicken. I had the chocolate cake and sandwiches. Ric and his mother were heavily laden.

We hurried toward the shady grove where there were picnic tables, hoping to get a table near the drinking water and restrooms. Mama and Ric's mother would spend the day here, gossiping with the other parents and guarding the food from ants. We kids ranged all over the amusement park, returning to the grove for food, or to rest, or to ask for more money.

Me and Ric headed for the shooting gallery. The sharp cracks of the .22 rifles hurried us along. We were surprised to find Batty Benson helping the owner. Batty started in the first grade with us, but he could never learn to read and dropped out of school after spending three years in the third grade. Miss Fannie just wouldn't ever pass him.

"Hi, Batty," Ric said. "How long you been working here?"

"Since Tolchester opened on Decoration Day," Batty said, and he picked up a rifle and aimed at a swinging target before pulling the trigger. When he hit the moving disk, a bell rang.

"Come over here everybody," Batty called. "Test your skill. Hit the moving target five times in a row and you will win a genuine U.S. cavalry revolver."

"Do they pay you for working here, Batty?" I asked.

"Sure, and I can shoot as many times as I want for nothing. Only thing I can't do is to win one of these big horse pistols."

"What does it cost to shoot this year, Batty?" Ric asked.

"Same as last year, three shots for a dime, ten for a quarter."

"Let's shoot ten times, Noah," Ric said, putting a quarter on the counter. "Maybe we can win one of those horse pistols."

I put a quarter down and Batty gave us rifles.

"Watch that middle pigeon in the second row," Ric said, and raised his rifle. When he pulled the trigger the pigeon disappeared.

I shot and hit a metal rabbit.

"Let's try the moving targets," Ric said. "They are the ones that ring the bell."

He carefully drew a bead on a flying duck, but he missed.

"You don't have to lead a swinging duck as much as a real duck, Ric," Batty said.

"I know that," Ric said, and shot at the flying duck again. This time he hit it and a bell rang.

I shot at a flying airplane and missed it twice.

Ric shot at the flying duck and missed. That made him mad and he fired the rest of his shots without hitting the duck again. I didn't do any better.

"Let's go over to the Whirlpool Dip, Noah," Ric said.

My stomach was just beginning to settle down after the ride in the automobile. I didn't want to ride on the roller coaster, but if I refused, Ric would say I was afraid.

On the way, we paused near the merry-go-round. Several of our Sunday School kids, mostly girls, were riding on the brightly painted carousel. Dora was sitting on a lion and Millie Robinson, who was also in our grade, was beside her riding a giraffe. As the merry-go-round slowed down, they waved at us.

"We don't want to waste our money on that hurdy-gurdy," Ric said. "It's for girls and little kids. Let's go over and take a ride on the Whirlpool Dip."

That strange feeling returned to my stomach. I was glad when Dora and Millie left the merry-go-round and joined us.

"Millie wants to ride on the Ferris wheel," Dora said, "but I'm afraid of high places."

"That's just your imagination, Dora," Ric said. "What could happen to you on the Ferris wheel?"

"The wheel might get stuck with me in the top car."

"I wouldn't mind being up there in the top car alone with you, Dora," Ric said.

But Dora took my arm as we strolled toward the Ferris wheel and that left Ric with Millie. After we bought the tickets, Dora couldn't back down. Soon we were high in the air, high enough to see the western shore of the Chesapeake Bay. Several large vessels were moving down the channel and smaller sailboats were reaching along the shore.

Dora was afraid to look down and grabbed my arm when the Ferris wheel stopped for a moment. But she soon got used to the wheel and insisted that we take another ride.

"Now we can go on the Whirlpool Dip," Ric said, after we left the Ferris wheel. "Do you girls want to join us?"

"You're not going to get me on the roller coaster," Dora said.

When a bell started to ring, Millie looked at her wristwatch. "It's twelve o'clock," she said, "and time for us to get our lunch."

Mama always says if you feel weak it's probably because you don't have any food in your stomach. It had been a long time since breakfast, so we hurried toward the picnic grove.

Mama and Ric's mother were spreading a large white table-cloth on the grass. The ants started to collect; it was our job now to drive them away. Dora and Millie returned to their families.

"See you later, alligator," Dora said as they walked away.

"She thinks she's smart," Ric said. "Wait until we get her on that roller coaster."

We started with sandwiches and moved on to the roasted chicken, with deviled eggs and olives to whet our appetites. The beaten biscuits were as hard as rocks, but after you cut one in half and butter it, you'll never really like a slice of bread again. Mama saved the chocolate cake for last and had some lemonade to go with it. She thought of everything and had even brought toothpicks.

"You're to rest in the shade for half an hour before running off again," she said, after we had finished eating.

Ric didn't like to have anybody telling him what to do. He looked at me and rolled his eyes, but his mother also insisted that we rest awhile.

When we saw Dora and Millie moving our way, they couldn't hold us any longer.

"I would certainly like to have a Kewpie Doll," Dora said, and Millie nodded her head in agreement.

"Have you forgotten we are on a Sunday School picnic?" Ric asked. "You wouldn't want us to gamble, would you?"

"Reverend Hammond won a doll this morning," Dora said. "Anyway, he was carrying one."

"Let's go over to the booth and see who's there," I said, so we moved that way. I could hear the clicking of the gambling wheel turning and the hawker shout:

"Come over here, everybody! Come over here, everybody! Round and round the big wheel goes and where it stops nobody knows. Step up gents and buy a paddle and win a Kewpie Doll for your sweetheart, mother, or sister."

Dora was walking with Ric and that left Millie with me. She wasn't as pretty as Dora; I wasn't figuring on spending much money on her.

When we came to the gambling wheel, there was PeeWee Sumner holding five paddles in each hand. The gambling wheel only had fifteen numbers. PeeWee's father must have given him twenty-five dollars to spend in Tolchester. A strange girl was standing beside PeeWee, her hand on his arm. She didn't belong in our Sunday School and looked like a city girl. PeeWee must have picked her up somewhere. Girls will go with anybody who has plenty of money.

"Turn the wheel, fellow," PeeWee said, "so that I can win a doll for this doll."

"Who'll buy the remaining paddles so somebody will be sure to win?" the gambler called, looking our way.

"Let's take them, Ric," I said, so we bought the five that were left and divided them.

But the wheel stopped at seven and that was one of PeeWee's numbers. While his girl was choosing a Kewpie Doll, he noticed us for the first time.

"Hello, suckers," PeeWee said. "How'd you like to have my system for beating the wheel? I'll tell you how to win a Kewpie Doll for a buck."

"You were just lucky," Ric said.

"It's not a matter of chance," PeeWee said. "It's like my old man says: 'It takes money to make money.'"

PeeWee and the girl strolled away and we continued to play the gambling wheel. I had to spend a dollar to win a Kewpie

Doll and gave it to Millie because she was holding my arm. Ric spent more than I did without winning anything.

"Let's go over to the Whirlpool Dip while we have some money left," he said.

As we approached the roller coaster, we could hear the screams of the riders and see the little cars racing up and down the hills before diving into the whirlpool with its dark tunnel. We walked over to the loading platform just as a car rolled in after making the run. PeeWee Sumner and his girl were in the front seat. The other passengers climbed out, but they remained.

"Let's take another ride, Clarissa," PeeWee said, giving the conductor two tickets.

"Step right up and buy your tickets," the conductor said, looking our way.

"No, thanks," Dora said, stepping back. "Just to watch the roller coaster speed up and down those hills scares me half to death."

"I never knew you were a scaredy-cat, Dora," Ric said. "How about you, Millie?"

"I'll go if Dora will," Millie said, squeezing my arm.

The conductor was holding the car with PeeWee and Clarissa in the front seat, waiting for us to make up our minds.

PeeWee must have overheard us. "Who's a sissy, now?" he called. "All four of you are sissies."

Dora was carrying an open parasol. Now she closed it with a bang. "All right," she said. "I'll go, but if I drop dead, don't forget I warned you."

We bought tickets and climbed aboard the roller coaster. The car slowly began to climb the first hill. It was a gentle one. Passing the top of the hill, it gained only a little speed on the way down.

"This isn't so bad, Dora, is it?" Ric shouted.

"You just wait," Dora called. "Look at that hill ahead."

Ric turned to us. "You kids can close your eyes if you can't stand it."

When the roller coaster reached the top of the hill, it paused for a moment, giving us time to look down the steep incline. It was much steeper than any of the hills where we coasted with our sleds.

"Hold your hats!" PeeWee shouted from the front seat and grabbed Clarissa as the little car plunged downward, its wheels whining on the wooden track.

Dora closed her eyes and screamed, grabbing Ric's arm. Millie screamed, too, but I kept my eyes open. I was so scared that my eyes were stuck and I couldn't close them. But I didn't scream—I had lost my voice, too. When we reached the bottom of the hill, I was surprised to see that Ric had his eyes closed.

"What's the matter, Ric?" I asked. "Are you scared, too?"

He opened his eyes and blinked. "What d'you mean?" he demanded. "I just had some grit in my eye."

Dora was watching him. "Listen to the brave man talk. Who's chicken now?"

We caught our breaths and tried to relax as the car slowly climbed the last and steepest hill; it loomed above the Ferris wheel.

"Oh, my," Dora cried, clinging to Ric's arm. "If I live through this, nobody will ever get me on a roller coaster again, not if I live to be a hundred."

On the top of the hill, the roller coaster stopped to give us an opportunity to view what was waiting ahead of us. I had a strong desire to climb out of the car when I looked down the steep incline to the pool of water below. Only Millie's hand clutching my arm prevented me.

The roller coaster plunged downward toward the pool of

water that from our height didn't look any bigger than the wash-tub I used on Saturday night. This time everybody in the car screamed; I could even hear Ric's budding bass voice. We all closed our eyes, too. I didn't open them until the splash when the car hit the water and slowed down. That sound of the water running along the car like it was a rowboat was a pleasant sound. When I opened my eyes, we were moving slowly through the dark tunnel that ended the ride. In the darkness, a fellow had a chance to do some necking while his girl was still too weak to resist him. I was still too scared to take advantage of the darkness, but I guess Ric tried. I heard Dora say something and a sound that must have been when she slapped Ric. Anyway, when the roller coaster suddenly emerged into the sunshine, he was rubbing his cheek. PeeWee collected; he and Clarissa were still necking when the car stopped at the loading platform. Dora was the first one to get off, and even Ric didn't insist on another trip. But PeeWee and Clarissa did.

We spent the last of our money to buy hot dogs and milk shakes, with the girls chipping in, and went down to the beach to watch the bathers. We stayed there for a long time, sitting in the sun and watching the fellows show off for the girls, until most of them had left the water and Millie looked at her wrist-watch.

"It's quarter to four," she said. "Reverend Hammond told us that the automobiles would leave for home at four o'clock."

When we returned to the picnic grove, Mama was already worrying about us. On our way home, I didn't notice how fast the automobile was traveling. The hum of the rubber tires on the asphalt road was soothing. After that ride on the Whirlpool Dip, the automobile seemed slow and safe.

10

🐚 All God's Children

When I *went uptown* to get a newspaper early Sunday morning, Mickey Salmons told me that Chautauqua had arrived. His
father was one of the men who persuaded the Chautauqua to
come to our town. They had to promise to buy so many season
tickets. An adult ticket cost two dollars. It admitted the bearer
to the afternoon and evening programs for the entire week, a
total of twelve. Children's tickets cost only one dollar. Besides,
the college boys in the tent crew conducted a class in gymnastics
for us boys. A lady conducted a class in handicrafts for the girls.
On the last day of Chautauqua, the girls exhibited what they
had made and we boys performed for our parents and friends.

"Let's go over and watch them put up the tent," Mickey
said.

Chautauqua had been coming to our town for several years.
I was glad to see Ron Harris again. This year, he was captain
of the tent crew. Last year I had stood on his shoulders and
someone had taken a picture of us. Another year and he would
be killed in an airplane crash in France—only I didn't know
that then. Now Ron was a senior at Swarthmore College and

ran the mile on the track team. After working all summer with Chautauqua, he and the other college boys were as brown as watermen. Their arm and leg muscles were hard from pitching the big tent in a dozen towns. All of the tent crew wore white sleeveless jerseys, white duck trousers, and white tennis shoes.

Ron remembered us. "Hi, kids. You're just in time to help us raise the tent. You can keep us supplied with pegs."

They had already stretched the tent on the playground in back of our school. The next step was to drive the pegs and tie the edges. The crew worked in pairs, each swinging a heavy maul to drive the pegs through the hard earth. It took a lot of strength to swing a maul. After all the pegs were driven, the lines along the outside of the tent were tied to the pegs. They used clove hitches, a knot we had learned in the Boy Scouts.

"We're going to need more men to raise the poles and the ceiling of the tent," Ron said.

"The school janitor might help," Mickey said, so we went off to find him.

When we returned with Mr. White, the tent crew had rounded up more helpers. All together we raised the heavy poles and tent. The poles were strengthened with guy ropes fastened to pegs. Outside, more pegs were driven and lines from the tops of the side walls were tied to them. By that time, we were ready to rest on the lawn.

"What are your best programs this year, Ron?" I asked.

"We've got a magician you kids will like. Wait until you see him saw a woman in half. He's an escape artist, too."

"You've got Houdini?" Mickey asked.

"No, but he's as good as Houdini."

"Pop says William Jennings Bryan is going to speak again," Mickey said.

"That's right," Ron said.

Several years ago, the great orator who had unsuccessfully run three times for president of the United States had spoken at the Chautauqua in our town. The tent was packed—even Dad had gone—and I had to sit on his knee. I was seven that summer. Then after President Wilson had appointed Bryan secretary of state, he had stopped speaking at Chautauqua. But soon after the sinking of the *Lusitania*, when the president wrote some stern notes to the German government, Bryan had resigned his cabinet post and now he was back on the Chautauqua platforms.

"What's he talking about?" Mickey asked.

"Mr. Bryan doesn't think we should do anything to involve our country in the European war," Ron said.

After resting, we walked toward home. "My father has pledged himself to buy twenty-five of the adult tickets," Mickey said.

Some years Mama bought one adult ticket, and she always managed to buy a children's ticket for me, even though I didn't attend all the programs. I never missed the morning class in gymnastics, where we learned to tumble, build pyramids, and wrestle Indian-style, but some of the afternoon and evening programs were so educational—long lectures about physics or moral talks by men who handled themselves like preachers. If they had a message, I was too sleepy to hear it. I never missed the three-act play or musical that was the feature of the week.

When I went home Mama wanted to know where I had been. She reached into her handbag and gave me the children's ticket for Chautauqua.

"Write your name on the back of it and put it in a safe place," she said.

"Is William Jennings Bryan speaking this year?" Dad asked.

"Sure," I said, "he's arguing that we should stay out of the war."

"Most of those westerners are isolationists," Dad said. "Europe must seem a long way off if you live in Nebraska."

"It can't be too far off for me," Mama said. "Thank the Good Lord Noah is not old enough to go, even if we get into it. Colin is talking about enlisting in the National Guard."

Colin is Ric's older brother. He's got even more nerve than Ric. He says the Germans haven't made the bullet that can kill him.

On Sunday afternoon, instead of playing baseball, we went to the Chautauqua grounds. A large stage had been erected at one end of the tent; it even had footlights, and electric lights had been strung for the evening programs. Everything was ready for a week of Chautauqua. The tent crew lived in a smaller tent they had pitched nearby. They were sitting on the lawn when we came along. Ron Harris was playing a guitar.

"I'm going to teach you how to do a somersault from my shoulders this year, Noah," he said. "What do you think about that?"

"It sounds like a good way to break my neck," I said, wondering what Mama would say if she heard about it.

"I'll hold onto your hands," Ron said.

Monday morning, when I came downstairs for breakfast, I was wearing the maroon and black athletic jersey that "Guts" Gordy had worn, the one with the number 13 on the back.

"I don't like to see you wearing that number thirteen, Noah," Mama said.

"Don't be superstitious, Evaline," Dad said. "You should trust more in the Good Lord."

"Call on somebody you know better, George," Mama said. "It don't do no good for Noah to tempt bad luck."

When I arrived at the playground, Ric and Mickey were already there, and by nine o'clock we had a dozen boys for the gymnastics class, including five who had not been with us last year. Ron turned them over to another college boy.

"You fellows already know something about gymnastics," he said. "This year I'm going to teach you some new tumbles and stands. Let's limber up first with some setting-up exercises."

We lined up and Ron stood in front of us, explaining and demonstrating each exercise before leading us, counting aloud to keep us together. We exercised our arms and legs, ending with ten pushups that left us breathless.

While we were resting, Ron taught us how to play a new game called Simon Says. While exercising, if Simon tells you to stop or begin a new exercise, you must do whatever he says. But if Simon does not tell you—the leader is Simon—you continue on doing whatever you are doing. If you move or stop moving when Simon does not tell you, that eliminates you from the game. The last one who remains in the game is the winner. He becomes the next Simon, at least that's the way we played the game.

Maybe you think that nobody could fool you, but after listening to Ron describe an exercise and give the command to start, it was easy to follow him—even if Simon didn't say so.

Ron had a hard time fooling Ric. After he had eliminated the rest of us, Ric remained. It looked like he would never fool him.

"We've played enough of Simon Says, fellows," Ron said. "Let's go over on the lawn and build pyramids."

When he walked away, the rest of us followed him, even Ric, without Ron saying, "Simon Says." That was the way he eliminated Ric.

With all of those exercises, I took a nap after lunch, just like Dad does every day when he comes home from the river.

Tuesday morning, we began tumbling. Ron started out with

single and double somersaults, followed by flip-flops. One fellow stretched on his back on the ground and the rest of us turned somersaults over him by placing our hands on his raised knees. The catcher helped us with an upward push of his hands. Because of his strength, Ric tossed the rest of us.

A boys' choir from a church in New York City was scheduled for that afternoon. While we were practicing tumbling, some of the choir boys came over and watched us. They looked like the fellows from Baltimore and Philadelphia who sometimes visit our town during the summer. They were paler than us; maybe they never got out much in the sun, or perhaps it was because they took a bath every day—the cities are so dirty. One of the city boys, he had red hair, was a smart-talker.

"What's your name, Mac?" he said to Ric.

When Ric didn't answer him, this same boy turned to the other choir boys. "The natives are not talking this morning," he said.

Ric still didn't say anything, but he got up and moved toward the redhead. Ron stopped him and ordered the choir boys to move on.

Some of those city boys may have been tough, but when they sang that afternoon, they were like a choir of angels. The redhead who talked smart to Ric sang a soprano solo that must have hit high C. He looked upward, toward the top of the tent on the highest notes and seemed about to fly away.

The choir boys sang one of the hymns we sang in our children's choir, "From Greenland's Icy Mountains," and a carol that we sang at Easter. But their best numbers were Negro spirituals, the same ones the colored folks in our town sing in their church when they have a week of revival meetings.

The boys' choir began with "Swing Low, Sweet Chariot," and ended with one called "I Got a Robe." That was the one I liked the most. It's first verse goes:

I got a robe, you got a robe;
All God's children got a robe;
When I get to Heaven goin' to put on my robe,
Goin' to shout all over God's Heaven.

The leader of the choir taught our audience the chorus and we all joined in, some even clapped their hands. I wished our children's choir would sing hymns like that sometimes.

Tuesday night, I went to Chautauqua again, just to hear the boys' choir. It was easier to believe in Heaven listening to those city boys sing.

Wednesday was a big day at Chautauqua for us boys. Blackstone the Magician took over the entire evening program. Most of us fellows could do card tricks. One Christmas, Aunt Carrie had given me a box of magic tricks that included a book telling how to become a magician. I mystified Mama and Dad before trying it on Ric and the others. There was a disappearing ball trick—the ball was fastened to a rubber band that I tied to the back of my pants. That didn't fool Ric for long. I could also make a card disappear from a hat and a coin disappear from a glass of water. What I really dropped into the glass was a glass disk. It sounded like a coin, but you couldn't see it. That even fooled Ric. After Aunt Carrie gave me the magic set, for a while I was thinking of becoming a magician. That was before the college coach gave me the maroon and black jersey that "Guts" Gordy had worn.

I could hardly wait for Wednesday night to arrive and went to the Chautauqua right after supper so as to be sure to get a seat up front close to the stage. If Blackstone used any wires to make objects fly through the air or disappear, I wanted to be close enough to see them. I found a seat in the front row next to PeeWee Sumner. He is such a pest that nobody wanted to sit next to him. Ric was on the other side of me.

PeeWee didn't attend the gymnastics class, but his father must have bought about one hundred tickets to the Chautauqua.

"Hi, shrimp," PeeWee said to me. I didn't like to be called shrimp, and I guess he didn't like to be called PeeWee.

"Hi, PeeWee," I said, turning toward Ric.

"Father says Blackstone is a fake," Peewee said. "Let's watch close and expose him."

It wasn't time for the show to start, but some of the magician's equipment was already on the stage. Included was a long black box that looked like a coffin and a big two-man wood saw.

"Let's put PeeWee in that box, Noah," Ric said, grinning. "After we saw him in half, his father can have staves made out of him for his basket factory."

"That's very funny," PeeWee said, "only nobody could get you and Noah on that stage—you're too scared of that."

"Keep on talking, PeeWee," Ric said, "and me and Noah will throw you up on that stage."

We might have if Blackstone hadn't walked out on the stage at that moment. He was wearing a long, flowing black cape that was big enough to conceal a horse. When he took off his tall silk hat, a rabbit jumped out.

"Anybody could hide a rabbit in that large a hat," PeeWee called, loud enough for Blackstone to hear.

But when a beagle rabbit hound jumped out of the same hat and chased the rabbit, I couldn't see how that big dog could have been concealed in the hat.

"You had the beagle concealed in your cape," PeeWee called, and this time I'm sure that Blackstone heard him. Anyway, he took off his cape. He was still wearing a long-tailed black coat that must have had a lot of secret pockets.

Blackstone took a pack of cards out of the air and began to mystify us. He made the cards disappear before our eyes, then found them again in back of his ears or in the air. Then he started to present the same card trick that Dad could do, at least it started out that way, until the magician made the ace of spades disappear entirely. He searched everywhere and couldn't find it. He stepped to the front of the stage and looked down on us boys—he could almost touch us with his wand. He acted like he thought one of us might have his ace of spades. His eyes focused on PeeWee just like Miss Fannie's do when she thinks we are concealing a comic book.

"Will you come up on the stage a minute, young man?" he said, pointing his wand at PeeWee, "and please bring my ace of spades with you."

PeeWee cringed when the magician pointed the wand at him. "I don't have your card, Mister."

"That's not what my wand tells me," Blackstone said. "Just step up onto the stage for a moment. I won't hurt you."

"Who's scared now, PeeWee?" I said.

When he stood up and moved toward the steps leading to the stage, everybody applauded. Blackstone searched PeeWee's pockets and even looked inside his mouth—it was big enough to conceal the card—but he didn't find his ace of spades.

PeeWee's father was sitting in the back of the tent. He stood up and called loud enough for everybody to hear. "Don't you think that you'd better apologize to my son, Blackstone?"

"Perhaps," the magician said, and asked PeeWee to take off his shoes. In one of them he found his missing ace of spades. He held it up so that everyone could see. That was a neat trick but PeeWee didn't like it.

"He must have palmed that card," he said, after returning to his seat.

After mystifying us with a number of small balls and silk flags, Blackstone clapped his hands and a dancing girl—she was dressed like the hoochy-koochy girls at the county fair—came out on the stage. We were close enough to see that she was not beautiful. The magician hypnotized her, or said he did, before opening the black box and helping her to climb inside. Then he closed the lid and locked it. He asked for someone from the audience to help him with his two-man saw, but even Ric wouldn't do that. So he called to the manager and he got Ron Harris to take the other end of the saw.

We could see the dancing girl's feet sticking out of holes in one end of the box and her hands sticking out of the other end. After oiling the saw, Blackstone and Ron sawed the box in half, and moved the two parts away from one another. Seeing the girl's feet ten feet away from her hands did something to my stomach. I didn't feel right until Blackstone put the box together again and unlocked it. When the magician lifted the lid, the girl jumped out without any help at all—she was all in one piece, too. Ric said that either the hands or feet we saw sticking out of the end of the box were fake ones—they had to be.

Even Dad went to Chautauqua on Friday night; that was the night William Jennings Bryan spoke. Dad had voted for him three times when he ran for president. On Friday night the tent was so crowded that the tent crew had to borrow more chairs from the undertakers. Even then a lot of the men stood up in the back of the tent.

While we were waiting for Bryan to appear, a thunderstorm began to build up in the northwest. It was one of those storms that can't make up its mind where to strike. It rumbled and rumbled and never seemed to get any closer.

"I left all my windows open," Mama said. "I hope Mrs. Steers will close them."

"We may not get this one at all," Dad said, "if it holds off until the tide changes."

"When does it change, Dad?" I asked.

"It's high water around nine o'clock."

William Jennings Bryan had arrived on the 7:04 train, and had gone to the Voshell House for supper and to meet with some of our Democratic leaders. While we were listening to the storm, he suddenly walked out on the stage. The crowd applauded and whistled—somebody even gave a rebel yell. In those days, almost everybody in our town voted the straight Democratic ticket. At political rallies, the band played Dixie.

William Jennings Bryan was fifty-three in 1916. He was still a handsome man, his hair streaked with gray, and when he started to speak I could understand why the newspapers said he had a silver tongue. Everybody was charmed, everybody but the thundergust—it had made up its mind and was heading our way and moving rapidly.

When Mr. Bryan urged us not to allow the politicians of any party to involve us in the European war that would send our American boys overseas to face the cannons of Europe, the thunder rolled and rumbled like the cannons might have been already here in America.

When the orator declared that no country anywhere in the world would dare to attack the United States, there was a flash of lightening and a hard clap of thunder, and all the lights went out. The people started to shout and a woman screamed. Fortunately, the lights came on again. Then it started to rain, torrents that found holes in the tent. Folks began to move their chairs searching for a dry spot until all the aisles were blocked.

William Jennings Bryan kept right on talking, loud as he could, but it was hard to hear what he was saying.

Things were bad enough, but when the wind arrived, it

looked like it might blow the tent down on all of us. I was watching the guy lines that supported the tent poles. They were tied to pegs, and as the water soaked into the ground, the pegs began to work loose. The tent crew must have also been watching the guy lines. They drove new pegs where the ground was still hard.

"Good Lord, George," Mama said, after she had regained herself. "Suppose this tent should fall down on our heads. How would we get out?"

"The worst is over," Dad said. "With as high a wind, the storm will soon be gone."

He was right. Soon the wind began to slacken and so did the rain. We could hear William Jennings Bryan's voice again as he finished his speech and sat down. We were ready to applaud, both for him and the end of the thundergust.

On Saturday afternoon, I somersaulted from Ron Harris's shoulders and almost scared Mama to death. That night we attended the last performance of Chautauqua; it was a Gilbert and Sullivan operetta, "The Mikado."

School opened on Monday morning. By that time, the Chautauqua tent had disappeared from our school grounds.

 New Girl

When I went home from school, Mama was talking to a new customer, a pretty lady whose name was Green. Her daughter, Clarissa—she was the girl with PeeWee Sumner at the Sunday School picnic—had just enrolled in our class. After Mrs. Green had gone, Mama cornered me.

"Is Clarissa pretty?" she asked.

"I guess so," I said.

"Her mother was the prettiest girl in town," Mama said. "She was Mary Tilghman and her father was the president of the bank—that was long before you came along. Mary was a wild girl and none of the local boys could interest her for long. Then one summer, she met a young chap from New York City and it was love at first sight. She had a big church wedding and they went away to live in New York. Last spring her husband was killed in an automobile accident and now Mary has opened the old Tilghman house on Water Street."

"Did she have much work for you?" I asked.

"I'm going to make new curtains for the house and some clothes for Clarissa, but you wouldn't be interested in them."

"No, ma'am," I said, wondering what kinds of female clothing Mama was making for Clarissa.

Having a new girl in our class caused all sorts of trouble. Ric and Alvin were smarter than usual, showing off for Clarissa, and she smiled and fluttered her eyelids in a way that encouraged them. Some of the older boys in high school began to hang around our homeroom until Miss Keen chased them away.

Clarissa and Dora were cousins. Mama always says that blood is thicker than water, but watching them I didn't get the idea that the two girls were the best of friends. Matters got worse after Clarissa took Ric away from Dora. They had been walking home together starting last spring, but the day after Clarissa arrived, Ric walked home from school with the new girl, carrying her books like he might have been her slave.

One morning Clarissa came to school wearing lipstick and Miss Keen sent her to the girls' room to wash it off. By that time none of the girls would have anything to do with Clarissa, but that made her more attractive to us boys. At recess time, when we played baseball, she joined us. One day, she hit a home run and lost our ball. That was the day Clarissa was at my house when I went home. Mama was fitting a dress on her and wouldn't let me in the house. I sat on the porch until Clarissa went home.

"Mary Tilghman's girl is just like her mother," Mama said to Dad while we were eating supper. "When I was her age, I was still a child. That girl acts like a young lady."

"You got married when you were sixteen, Evaline," Dad said.

"Clarissa is Noah's age, going on fourteen," Mama said. "He's still a child and she's almost grown."

"I'm as tall as Clarissa," I said.

"I wasn't thinking just of size," Mama said, turning to Dad.

"That girl is already thinking of marriage, George. This afternoon she asked me if it wasn't just as easy to love a rich man as a poor man."

Since none of the girls would mix with Clarissa, she began to play with us boys on Saturdays. When we played Run, Sheep, Run, she ran and hid with us. One day Clarissa stepped on a rock and twisted her ankle. We thought she would cry, but she swore instead. But it was awkward sometimes when we climbed a tree or a ladder until Clarissa turned up one Saturday wearing bloomers under her dress. Before that she had worn drawers just like the other young females.

"Is Clarissa wearing the bloomers I made for her?" Mama asked one Saturday afternoon after I came home from playing Run, Sheep, Run.

"Yes, ma'am," I said.

"Does she wear them in school, too?" she asked.

"I don't know," I said, thinking that Mama was getting awfully nosy.

"Mary had me make Clarissa's dresses two inches shorter than the patterns called for," Mama said. "She'd be more respectable wearing bloomers."

"Short skirts is a good way to catch a man," Dad said, "along with fancy lace on drawers."

"Nobody asked you for your opinion, George," Mama said.

What Dad said had a lot of truth in it. The boys were certainly interested in Clarissa, and she even flirted with our principal when he asked her how she liked our school.

"The boys keep teasing me and say something is wrong with my eyes," Clarissa said, fluttering her eyelids and smiling so as to show all of her teeth.

Mr. Manning was taken in, too. He moved closer so as to examine Clarissa's eyes, looking into their depths.

"There's nothing wrong with your eyes," he said. "I don't know why the boys should tease you. You look just right to me."

It was those last six words that did it. For a moment, we thought that Clarissa was going to fall into our principal's arms.

Mr. Manning was smiling; that was a rare sight for us. It was hard to tell which one had the biggest crush.

After Clarissa entered our class, the other girls began to shorten their skirts—even the ones with knobby knees—and act differently toward us boys. One day Dora came to school wearing lipstick and smelling like she had been into her mother's perfume. She walked past Ric's desk several times during the homeroom period. If Miss Keen saw the lipstick, she didn't say anything to Dora about it. The next day, most of the girls were wearing lipstick.

On Saturday, when we gathered to play Run, Sheep, Run, Clarissa was missing.

"I saw her walking along Water Street with PeeWee Sumner," Ric said, "arm in arm—it was sickening."

"That must have been them walking across the bridge a few minutes ago," Mickey said.

We chose sides and gave the sheep ten minutes start before chasing them. I was one of the wolves and ran across the bridge hoping to spy Clarissa and PeeWee, but they had disappeared. We never did find any of the sheep, and when the twelve o'clock whistle blew on the basket factory, we called "All in" several times and went home to lunch.

That afternoon when I went down to the river, several of the gang were there. Clarissa was still missing. Then PeeWee came along riding his bicycle.

"Where were you and Clarissa all morning?" Ric demanded. "Are you trying to break up our game?"

"We took a long walk together," PeeWee said, looking sort of moon-faced like he had seen a vision.

"Where's Clarissa?" Billy asked.

"I took her home." PeeWee said. "She's breaking out with poison ivy or something. We were in Klinefeller's Woods."

"What were you doing in the woods?" Erny asked, grinning.

"Just picking flowers and horsing around," PeeWee said.

"Maybe that's not all you were doing," Ric said, and he wasn't grinning.

"Clarissa is not like other girls," PeeWee said. He really had it bad.

When I went home to supper, Mama already knew about Clarissa and PeeWee taking a walk alone in the woods.

"That girl is as fast as her mother was," she said, "seducing young boys with little thought of what might happen to her or them. And she would pick the son of the richest man in town. Don't let her tempt you, Noah."

When I went to school Monday morning, both Clarissa and PeeWee were absent. Ric had seen PeeWee Sunday afternoon and said he was also broken out with poison ivy or something. They both must have got it in Klinefeller's Woods, only by that time there was gossip that they had some kind of a disease that nobody would talk about—they would only hint.

On Wednesday, Clarissa and PeeWee came back to school. Their faces and arms and legs were covered with red splotches from the poison ivy—that's what it really was—but nobody was very sorry for them. When Mama heard about it, she said it served them right.

Clarissa was not attractive with the red splotches and the white salve she put on them. The rest of the girls must have been glad. But it's funny about girls. After the first day or two, they began to sympathize with Clarissa, and by the time Christmas arrived, she was one of their gang, too.

12

🐚 *Grandpappy's Final Hour*

January was cold with ice on the river. Saturday afternoon, when Dad came home, I could see he was worrying about something without him saying a word. So could Mama.

"What's the matter, George?" she asked. "Did you lose all your money playing poker with your lawyer friends?"

"Pap is sick," Dad said, "and this time it's bad. When I dropped in to see if he needed anything this afternoon, he was complaining of his leg and must have been running a fever. He kept asking me to tow his ark down the river to the Cliffs, and here it is only late January."

"Sounds like he has a high fever," Mama said, "wanting to go down the river in January. Even when he was younger, he never moved his ark until May."

"He kept saying we are going to have an early spring, and thinks if he can get his leg in salt water, it will soon be all right again," Dad said. "He thinks it's rheumatism, but it's liable to be something worse. Diabetes runs in my family. His father died of it when he was Pap's age."

"Did you take him to see Dr. Salmons?" Mama asked.

"You know how Pap feels about doctors," Dad said. "Besides, he can hardly walk."

"Can he get around enough to feed himself?" Mama asked.

"He ain't eating right."

"I've been cooking a pot of soup all afternoon," Mama said. "Noah, put on your coat and hat and take some over to your grandfather. It is made with a meat bone and will strengthen him."

Mama put the soup in a saucepan with a lid on it, and I carried it over to where Grandpappy lived on Water Street. Everything was quiet outside his ark and when I rapped on the door, nobody answered. So I rapped again and this time Grandpappy heard me.

"Come in," he said.

Grandpappy was stretched on his bunk with his glasses on, reading the morning newspaper. He never has much money, but he always manages to get daily and Sunday copies of the *Sun*. When he saw me, he dropped the newspaper on the floor.

"I thought you was Dr. Salmons," he said. "That's why I didn't answer right away. It would be just like your ma to send Puss Salmons down to see me."

"Mama sent you this vegetable soup, Grandpappy," I said, placing the saucepan on top of his pot-bellied stove to heat.

"Just like her," he said. "You know what a woman is, any woman? She's half an angel and half a devil—they're all like that."

"You were married to one for a long time, Grandpappy," I said.

"Thirty-five years come next April until pneumonia carried my Lizzie away," he said. "I made up my mind never to marry again. She was mostly angel with only a trace of the devil."

"What's the matter with your leg, Grandpappy?" I asked.

"I told your father it was only rheumatism, boy," he said. "George is gentle like his mother, and I didn't want to worry him. You are harder, more like your ma and me. I can tell you— my leg is rotting from diabetes, just like my pa's did when he was my age."

"Maybe Doctor Salmons could cure it," I said.

"I'm figuring on dying in one piece," Grandpappy said. "Nobody is going to strap me to a table and saw my leg off. Anyway, I'm about ready to go. I've been lonely for Lizzie lately."

I didn't like to hear Grandpappy talk like that. I figure we all have to go sometime, and he was getting along and no longer a spring chicken, but it wasn't pleasant talk.

"I've got to be getting on home, Grandpappy," I said. "Dad will stop by tomorrow to see how you're feeling."

"Nobody stays put long nowadays, boy," he said. "The world left me far behind long ago, and I ain't ever wanted to catch up with it."

When I got home Mama and Dad wanted to know what Grandpappy had said. I told them.

"It's the first time he's mentioned my mama in years," Dad said.

"Sounds like he's preparing himself to die," Mama said.

The next morning I went to church with Mama and Dad went down to see Grandpappy. We got home from church ahead of Dad. Mama was putting our dinner on the table when I saw him round the corner, walking faster than he usually did.

"Pap is worse," Dad said. "I got Doc Salmons to go down and look at him. He says Pap is in the last stages of diabetes and can't last more than a week or two. He wants me to put Pap in a hospital, but you know how he is. Pap says he's not afraid to die, but he wants to be with his own kin. He don't want to pass on among strangers."

"Blood is thicker than water," Mama said. "We'll put him in Noah's room. You can sleep on the couch, Noah. Who's with your father now, George?"

"Joe Meekins is sitting with him, but I told Pap I'd be back soon with a carriage to fetch him."

"I'll get Noah's room ready while you go and get him," Mama said.

While Dad was gone she put clean sheets and pillow cases on my bed, and I moved my clothes to the hall closet. Mama was making a fresh pot of coffee when I heard the crunch on the oyster shell road and went out to help Dad. I hitched the horse to a post while he was helping Grandpappy into the house.

When I followed them inside, Grandpappy was sitting at the kitchen table and Mama was pouring him a cup of coffee. His face was pink from the cold air, or it may have been the fever. He didn't look as sick as he was.

"I brought you a present, Evaline," Grandpappy said. "Go out to the carriage, Noah, and get my blue ginger jar. Be careful not to drop it."

I brought the ginger jar in and placed it on the table so we could see the man fishing.

"I want you to have it, Evaline," Grandpappy said. "My brother John brought it home to Lizzie years ago. It came all the way from Japan and once had a top, but somebody broke it."

Mama thanked Grandpappy and placed the blue ginger jar on the mantel by the clock.

We had our Sunday dinner, but Grandpappy didn't have much appetite. Dad helped him upstairs to my room as soon as he finished. I had to hurry not to be late for Sunday School. When I came home, Dad was resting on the couch and Mama was reading.

"How's Grandpappy?" I asked.

"He's been sleeping for most of the afternoon, and talking in his sleep," Mama said. "He's burning up with fever and thinks I'm his dead wife, Lizzie."

I had to go upstairs to put my coat away in the closet and tiptoed so as not to bother Grandpappy, but he heard me.

"Is that you, Lizzie?" he called. "Why is supper so late?"

"It's me, Grandpappy," I said.

He glared at me, his eyes red with fever, and for a moment didn't know me. Then his eyes cleared a bit. "It's Noah, come to see how his old Granddaddy is feeling."

"Yes, sir," I said.

"Where's that son of mine?" he demanded. "Like as not, he's asleep somewhere."

"Do you want to see him?" I asked.

He didn't seem to hear me. "What day is it, boy?" he asked.

"Sunday."

"Did you get a newspaper, today? I'd like to read it."

"Yes, sir," I said, and got him the *Sunday Sun* and his glasses, but by that time his mind was somewhere else.

"Tell your father I want to see him," he said.

When I woke Dad, he went upstairs right away. Mama and I could hear them talking.

"Seems like I'm already beginning to wear out my welcome in your home, George," Grandpappy said. "Today is Sunday but tomorrow is a working day. Tomorrow I want you to tow me and my ark down the Chester River to the Cliffs where the water is saltier. I've got a lot of friends there who will be right glad to see me. That salt water will fix my leg in a jiffy."

"You're talking crazy, Pap," Dad said. "Evaline and me are glad to have you here—you can stay as long as you like. You know there's ice on the river. Like as not we're going to have a couple of more cold spells before another spring."

"A son calling his Pa crazy," Grandpappy said. "You and Evaline are already scheming to put me in the lunatic asylum."

Dad called Mama, but she couldn't talk any sense into him. He finally wore himself out and went to sleep, but in the middle of the night I awoke when he cried out. Mama and Dad talked to him for a long while.

The next morning, while I was eating breakfast, Grandpappy started calling for his dead wife again. I left for school while Mama was trying to quiet him. When I came home at noon, Dr. Salmons was sitting in the parlor with Mama, writing a prescription. Dad was upstairs with Grandpappy.

"Now you know why I wanted to send James to the hospital," Dr. Salmons said. "At times he is going to be out of his head from now to the end. If he were in a hospital, a nurse could quiet him with a needle. This prescription I'm giving you contains morphine. It will deaden the pain in his leg and put him to sleep for a while. When he starts getting excited, give him one pill, but don't repeat the dose until at least four hours have elapsed. And keep the bottle out of his reach."

Mama gave me the prescription to take to the drugstore. When the druggist read it, you could tell by his face that he knew somebody was really ill. "I'll fill this right away," he said, and returned in a few minutes with a bottle of pills. "Keep this away from small children," he warned.

By the time I got home Grandpappy really needed one of the pills, but it took both Mama and Dad to get him to take it.

"I know what you and Puss Salmons are planning to do," Grandpappy said. "After I take one of them pills and it puts me to sleep, you'll cart me away to the lunatic asylum."

"It'll put you to sleep, Pap," Dad said, "and ease your pain, but when you wake up again, you'll be right here with us."

"And you'll be feeling better, Pap," Mama said.

"My leg is paining me something awful," Grandpappy said. "It would be worth most anything to get away from the pain. All right, give me one of them pills."

Mama took one out of the bottle and held the glass of water to help him swallow it. That morphine must be powerful. You could see it take effect on Grandpappy in a few seconds. Mama arranged the pillows to make him more comfortable, and he went to sleep, smiling that quiet smile of his. I wondered what he was dreaming about.

"You haven't had any lunch yet, Noah," Mama said. "You must be half-starved."

Dad sat with Grandpappy while Mama got me some food. I was late for school and she wrote me an excuse for Mr. Manning. When I came home again, Grandpappy was still asleep and Mama was working in the kitchen.

"Your father has been upstairs ever since you left, Noah," she said. "Take his place for a while."

I went upstairs and found Dad asleep in the rocking chair. When I touched his shoulder he awoke and left me alone with Grandpappy. He was breathing. I could see his chest slowly rising and falling. Then he opened his eyes and saw me.

"I caught you this time, boy," he whispered, "spying on your old granddaddy."

"Do you want anything, Grandpappy?" I asked.

"Nothing now, boy. Maybe later, Evaline will give me another pill. My what a dream I've just had. Where do you think I've been, boy?"

"Maybe you dreamed you were fishing for perch under the bridge," I said, knowing it was one of his favorite spots.

"No, sir," he said. "I just dreamed I was in Heaven and saw Lizzie there, along with a lot of my old friends I weren't sure would ever make it. It's a wonderful place, Heaven. I'd always had my doubts when the preacher said there were pearly gates and streets paved with gold, but it's so, boy."

I wondered who else he had seen, but I didn't like to ask him.

"I didn't have any trouble getting in," Grandpappy said. "When I rapped on those pearly gates, they opened up right away and there was St. Peter, standing with folded wings."

"'I've been expecting you for several days, James Marlin,' he said. 'Come inside out of the draft.' Then he took my measurement for a pair of wings."

"'Your wife, Lizzie, is anxious to see you, James,' St. Peter said."

"'How is Lizzie, St. Peter,' I asked."

"'You know how women get at times, James,' he said. 'Lately, she's been lonely for her earth-neighbors. She's not very happy here.'"

"That seemed queer, not to be happy in Heaven," Grandpappy said. "It was sure a pretty place."

"'I'll take you to see Lizzie, right away,' St. Peter said, giving me a harp to strum."

"We flew right down the main street, moving like a couple of wild swan, our necks outstretched as we looked for Lizzie."

"St. Peter was the first to spot her, in the middle of a large crowd of the dear departed. They were all dressed like they were mourning something. They were moaning and crying and quite unhappy, even though they had made it past the pearly gates. I recognized a lot of them as former Eastern Shoremen."

"'Why are these redeemed folks so unhappy, St. Peter?' I asked."

"He shrugged his wing. 'Ask your wife,' he said."

"Lizzie was glad to see me, but she was also sorrowing for something else."

"'What's wrong, Lizzie?' I asked. 'Here you've made it, and now I've joined you, and still you look like a hound that's lost all of her pups.'"

"'Oh, Jimmy,' she said. 'Heaven is a fine place with a lot of modern conveniences, but we country folks would all rather go home where we belong in our earthly paradise on the Eastern Shore.'"

When I told Mama and Dad about Grandpappy's dream, Mama went next door to see Mrs. Steers. She had a dream book that can tell you what any dream really means. Soon Mama was back again.

"He's preparing himself to die," she said.

"Don't forget those pills Doc Salmons gave him," Dad said. "They ought to give him all kinds of dreams. Anyway, I'm glad he thinks he's going to Heaven."

That evening, Mama gave Grandpappy another pill that kept him asleep for most of the night. Until about six o'clock in the morning, just before light, I heard him arguing with Dad. Grandpappy wanted to go back to his ark.

When I came home from school for lunch, Doctor Salmons and Mama were sitting in the parlor.

"His heart is beating like a young man's," the doctor said. "He just won't give up and die, talked to me about going down the river in his ark when he felt better."

"How long can this go on, Doctor?" Mama asked.

"It can't be longer than a few days, and it might come at any time," Doctor Salmons said. "Give him the pills to deaden the pain and keep him quiet, but space them as far apart as you can, or he might go to sleep and not awaken again."

"That might be for the best," Mama said.

It was like that all week with Grandpappy sometimes out of his mind and other times just like he had always been. On

Saturday morning, Mama had to go to the meat market; she likes to choose the meat herself. Dad had gone to the river to check his bateau, so I was left alone with Grandpappy.

"He'll probably sleep all the time I'm gone," Mama said on her way out the door. "I gave him a pill only about an hour ago, so don't give him another one, not even if he should ask you for one."

I stayed downstairs in the parlor where I could read the Book of Knowledge, close to the stairs so I could hear Grandpappy if he wanted anything. I was reading about Bonnie Prince Charlie when he awoke.

"Evaline," Grandpappy called, weak but clear, and when she didn't answer, "George, come here."

"I'm here, Grandpappy," I answered and went upstairs. He had pulled the covers back like he was about to get out of bed.

"Where are the others?" he asked, breathing hard.

I told him.

"My old heart is beginning to miss," Grandpappy said, "like the engine in George's bateau when it has a leaky gasket. Only Puss Salmons can't put a new gasket in my heart. Prop me up, Noah."

While I was putting the pillows in back of him, I could see his pulse beating in his neck; it was racing and skipping and missing beats like it was about to stop.

"Maybe I'd better go and get the doctor," I said.

Grandpappy took a deep breath. "There's a pain in my chest like nothing I ever had before."

"Mama will be home soon," I said.

"She'd better hurry, boy," Grandpappy said, and he reached over to grasp my hand.

"Maybe I'd better get the doctor," I repeated.

"It's too late for that," Grandpappy said, holding fast to my hand. "Don't grieve too much for me, boy. I've lived the way I wanted to live, leastwise during the last ten years since Lizzie passed on. Not many men have ten years to do as they please. I'd had time to read the newspaper every day, and the books I've wanted, and to go fishing when the perch were biting under the bridge." He paused to get his breath. "Folks like Eben Pauley call me shiftless, but I figure he and his stripe are the shiftless ones—so shiftless with the freedom our country promised everybody. Pretty soon everyone will be jumping and running to the bells and whistles—and for what purpose?"

The talking had exhausted Grandpappy. His eyes were brighter than I had ever seen them, but his hand in mine was as cold and clammy as a dead fish in January.

I heard the front door open and close. "Mama," I called, "Grandpappy is worse."

She took one look at him and sent me to get Doctor Salmons. He had office hours on Saturday morning, but he left his patients and came right away in his Dodge auto. I rode beside him in the front seat.

We were too late. Grandpappy had died a few minutes after I left to get the doctor, with Mama holding his hand.

"He passed on easy, Doctor," Mama said.

"It's often that way," Doctor Salmons said, closing Grandpappy's eyes. "Death is a release for many people."

Dad came home while Mama and the doctor were talking. He looked at Grandpappy and covered him with a sheet.

"Pap is past all pain, now," he said, and there were tears in his eyes. It was the only time I ever saw Dad cry—we're not the kind of folks who cry easily.

Mama made a pot of coffee and we all had a cup, even Doctor Salmons. He and Grandpappy had started out in the first grade together.

Just before noon, the undertaker and his helper arrived, wearing black derby hats, and carried Grandpappy away. When they brought him back, he was resting in a fine coffin, almost as big as his skiff. They had dressed Grandpappy in his best clothes and even given him a haircut and shave. He looked better than I'd ever seen him before.

When Dad came home he was wearing a new black hat with a broad brim—for a moment I didn't recognize him. Dad said Grandpappy looked fine. But Mama didn't like me looking at him, and sent me out to play. When I went home, a long black crepe was hanging on the front door, so I went in the back way.

The funeral was the next day. Grandpappy hadn't been to church for years, but when he was younger, he had sung in the choir of the Methodist church, so one of their preachers conducted the services. Our parlor was so crowded that some folks had to sit in the dining room.

The preacher delivered a sermon. He said Grandpappy was now safe in Heaven so there was nothing for the rest of us to worry about. After he finished, some of our neighbors carried Grandpappy out to the hearse. Dad had hired a hack from Greenley's Livery Stable to take us to the graveyard. But at the last moment Mama decided it would be better for me not to go. She put her hand on my forehead.

"You're running a temperature, Noah," she said. "You don't have to go to the graveyard. We'll be home soon."

Mama wanted to spare me the chill of seeing them put Grandpappy in the cold ground. She meant right, but after they had all gone, it was awfully quiet in the house. The smell of the funeral wreaths lingered; it was a sickening smell. I opened the back door and looked toward the river. The cove was covered with ice. The ground was stiff as a board. It must have been hard to dig Grandpappy's grave.

13

🐚 In Search of Arbutus

February was colder than January. After the river froze solid, the *B. S. Ford* stopped her daily runs to Baltimore. Almost every day we skated on the cove. Toward the end of the month, an icebreaker cut a channel from the bay to our town. In early March, the ice softened and we put away our skates.

One morning a dandelion was blooming in our front yard. On the way to school, Dora Tilghman came out of her house just in time to join me.

"I'll bet the pink arbutus is blossoming in the woods," she said. "Let's ask Miss Keen if she will take our class on a hike in the woods to pick the arbutus."

It's the first of our wild flowers to bloom.

"Now's the time," I said. "After the ground thaws, we'd sink in up to our knees in mud near the branch."

"Miss Keen is young enough to go with us," Dora said. "You talk to the boys and I'll mention it to the girls. Then during afternoon homeroom period, we'll ask Miss Keen."

That morning, we seventh graders were noisier than usual; we didn't settle down until the Bible was read.

"It's the spring that makes you so restless," our teacher said. "I'm still young enough to know how you feel. This kind of a day, I feel like playing hooky myself."

"You feel that way, too, Miss Keen?" Ric asked.

"Of course," she said. "Teachers are human, too."

Playing hooky wasn't anything to even talk about. Anybody caught would have a good chance of feeling Mr. Manning's big ruler on the seat of his breeches, along with another whipping from his father when he went home. Still in the early spring, somebody was bound to skip school or try to.

A week before, on the first really warm afternoon, PeeWee and Clarissa were both absent. The next morning, Clarissa brought a note signed by her mother saying she had been ill. PeeWee was in the eighth grade; we didn't know what excuse he had. Whatever it was, it didn't satisfy Mr. Manning, so he stopped in to see Mrs. Sumner on his way home from school. It turned out that PeeWee and Clarissa had played hooky together and gone off to Klinefeller's Woods in the pony cart that Mr. Sumner had given him for Christmas.

Since Clarissa was a girl, Mr. Manning couldn't whip her, and he didn't whip PeeWee either. Dad said it was because his father is the richest man in town. Mr. Sumner didn't whip PeeWee. Instead, he took away his Chincoteague pony, Buck, along with the cart and sold them to punish PeeWee for playing hooky.

If PeeWee loved anything, it was his pony. He took care of Buck himself, feeding and watering the pony. He curried and combed Buck and even cleaned out his stall—that's hard, dirty work.

Some folks said Mr. Sumner got rid of the pony and cart so as to have more room for his new automobile. It was a Stutz Bearcat and could go seventy-five miles an hour. He had bought the auto as a Christmas present for his wife, but she was afraid to drive it. Folks said Mr. Sumner thought more of his new automobile than he did of his wife or son. Most of the gossip was jealous talk—the Sumners now had two automobiles when hardly anybody else even had one.

During the morning recess, I mentioned Dora's idea of a nature hike to Ric and some of the other fellows.

"The arbutus doesn't interest me much," Ric said, "but anything that could get us out of school is worth trying. Maybe we could get the whole afternoon off."

"Mr. Manning wouldn't let us do that," I said.

I was on my way home at noon when Dora caught up with me. "Did you talk to the boys about our nature hike?" she asked.

"Ric thinks we should try and get the whole afternoon off," I said.

"That Ricard," Dora said. "You might think we are in jail. Mr. Manning wouldn't approve of that."

"That's what I told Ric," I said.

"If Ricard gets stubborn and argues, Miss Keen won't even consider it." Dora said.

When I went back to school after lunch, Dora had cornered Ric and was talking to him.

"Dora says half an apple is better than none, Noah," Ric said. "I still think it would be great to have the whole afternoon off. Just last week Miss Keen was explaining how we live in a democracy where things are decided by a majority of votes. If we all stick together, she would have to agree."

"Miss Keen is not that democratic, Ricard," Dora said.

"If we were excused for the afternoon, all the other kids would want off, too," I said.

Ric began to yield. "I hadn't thought of that," he said. "Even if he let us go, the other kids would call us teacher's pets."

"I'm going to mention the nature hike in homeroom, Ricard," Dora said. "Please don't ruin everything."

Ric liked to have Dora beg him. "All right, Dora, I'll try to keep my mouth shut."

When the warning bell rang, we went to our homeroom. After Miss Keen checked the roll, there was still five minutes left before afternoon classes. Dora raised her hand.

"Yes, Dora," Miss Keen said.

"You were telling us this morning how restless you feel in the spring, Miss Keen," Dora said. "Some of us have been wondering if you would like to take our class on a nature hike to the woods to pick the arbutus and other wild flowers."

While Dora was talking, I was looking out the window where the bare maples were turning red as their buds swelled.

"That's a good idea, Dora," our teacher said, "although I suspect that the boys would be more interested in watching the birds and wild animals than picking flowers. But when would we go? By the time school is dismissed, the sun is low. It would be dark before we reached the woods."

I could see Ric was about to speak and raised my hand. "You have us in science the next to the last period, Miss Keen. Isn't studying birds and flowers a part of science?"

"It certainly is," Miss Keen said, "but what about the last period?"

"We have physical education then," Dora said. "Wouldn't a long walk be good exercise?"

"That makes sense to me," Miss Keen said, "but I'll have to get Mr. Manning's permission."

The next morning, Millie Robinson, who lived on a farm near town, brought a bouquet of pussy willows to school. Her face was pink from the long walk in the cool air.

Miss Keen was pleased and gave Millie a vase to fill with water.

"I saw some white blossoms in the woods on the way to school," Millie said.

"That was shadbush," our teacher said. "It blossoms before the dogwood."

Even Ric and Alvin looked at the pussy willows. Several buds had burst and the flowers, looking like the paws of kittens, were coming out.

"Arbutus blossoms at the same time as pussy willows," Dora said. "Mother told me that."

"Have you asked Mr. Manning if we can go, Miss Keen?" Alvin asked.

"Not yet," our teacher said, "but I have an appointment to see him during my free period this morning."

During the afternoon homeroom period, we could hardly wait for Miss Keen to finish checking the attendance. It seemed she would never put the register in the drawer. When she did, several of us raised our hands.

"What did Mr. Manning say, Miss Keen?" Dora asked.

When our teacher stood up, she didn't have to wait for us to become quiet. You could have heard a pin drop. "Mr. Manning has given us his permission to take the nature hike, with certain provisions," she said.

Our class buzzed with excitement before becoming quiet again.

Ric raised his hand. "What provisions?" he asked.

"All of you will have to bring a note from a parent granting permission for you to go," Miss Keen said.

"That's O.K.," Dora said, and the rest of us nodded our heads.

"And we have to be home before sundown, by 6 p.m. at the latest," our teacher added.

"What day are we going?" Alvin asked.

"Mr. Manning thinks that Friday afternoon will be the best time. That will give you enough time to get permission from your parents and to make plans."

When I went home, I told Mama about our nature hike to the woods.

"What won't you younguns think of next," she said. "Like as not you talked your teacher into it. But it is nice to walk in the woods in the early spring and listen to the birds sing. You be sure to bring your mother a sprig of arbutus."

"Then you'll give me a note with your permission?" I said.

"I suppose so," she said, "only right now I'm doing some spring cleaning and have a number of chores for you."

I used my wagon to take a load of tin cans and other junk to the town dump. When I returned, Mama sat down and wrote the note.

The next morning, more than half our class brought notes and we decided where we were going—to the woods that stretch between Brewster's Cove and the Great Marsh. That was Wednesday. By Thursday, everyone had brought a note except Clarissa. Her mother decided to keep her home as a punishment for playing hooky with PeeWee the week before.

I went to bed early Thursday evening and awoke in the dawn to hear a wren singing near my window. The wren sings all winter during the warm days. It was a good sign that the day was going to be a good one. On the way to school, I saw a robin running across a lawn.

The morning passed slowly. When I went home for lunch, Mama made me put on my rubber shoes.

"The ground is still damp," she said. "Don't you try to cross the branch in Brewster's Woods. There are holes deep enough to drown a cow."

After lunch, we seventh graders had English. That period was the longest we had all year. When the bell rang, we put on our coats and hats and met Miss Keen and Mr. Manning on the front steps.

"I have a few words to say to you before you go, children," our principal said. "This nature hike is new for our school, and the way it turns out will largely decide whether I give other classes permission for trips during school hours. Do whatever Miss Keen says and keep close together."

Mr. Manning returned to his office, and we started for Brewster's Woods—it was about two miles from our school. We walked in twos and threes along the brick pavement until we came to the oyster shell road that led toward the woods. We paused to rest on the bridge over the creek and looked toward the river. Red-winged blackbirds were riding the marsh reeds; a fish hawk soared high over the river.

In town, Miss Keen had led the way, but now we boys ranged ahead. Ric shouted when he jumped a rabbit from a ditch. We chased the rabbit for a hundred yards before waiting for the others.

Miss Keen had Millie make a list of all the birds we saw. By the time we reached the woods, this included: a fish hawk, robins, red-winged blackbirds, cardinals, two mockingbirds, several kinds of woodpeckers, crows, buzzards, a marsh hawk and two large birds high in the sky Ric said were the bald eagles that live in the Great Marsh.

The girls were looking for violets and buttercups, but it was too early for them—all they found was dandelions until we came to the woods where brown leaves covered the ground. The leaves were dry and rustled as we moved under the trees. And under the leaves we found a few red partridge berries that the winter birds had overlooked.

We were after arbutus and pushed deeper into the woods where the white blossoms of the shadbush made it seem like a fairyland. Alvin was about to break a branch of the white blossoms when Miss Keen stopped him.

"You might hurt the shadbush, Alvin," she said. "Anyway the blossoms are so fragile that they wouldn't last until we get back to town."

We came to a gully that had a small stream running down the middle. "This is where we found arbutus last year," Millie said. "Look on the south side of the trees."

We spread out and moved along the gully. Millie was the first to find the arbutus, half-hidden by the brown leaves. She called to the rest of us and we ran to see. The girls stooped to sniff the flower's fragrance.

"It's a shame to pick it," Dora said. "It's so beautiful."

"If one of you girls don't pick it, I will," Ric said, so Millie picked the pink blossoms and gave them to Miss Keen.

"Let's not take all the arbutus we find," our teacher said. "We should leave some for next year."

In searching for the arbutus, we drifted apart, and Dora followed me along a path that led away from the gully.

"Where are you going, Noah?" she asked. "Mr. Manning told us to stay together."

"I want to show you something," I said, searching the side of the path for an opening until I saw a way through the briar and underbrush and left the path. Dora followed me. When I stopped, we could no longer hear the shouts of our classmates.

"We'll get lost, Noah," Dora said, giggling, but keeping close to me, "like Tom Sawyer and Becky Thatcher were."

"They were lost in a cave," I said. "Come on, I've got something to show you."

When we came to the edge of the branch, our search ended.

In the wet soil, fed by warm springs, clusters of violets were blossoming weeks ahead of their season. Neither of us said a word—we just stood and looked. Dora did stoop to sniff their fragrance, but she didn't pick a single violet. Then we heard Miss Keen calling for us and ran to join the others. We didn't tell them about the violets. They were our secret.

14

❧ On Dead Man's Curve

After the long walk to Brewster's Woods, I didn't stir after supper. Dad went uptown to get the newspaper. In February, the German subs had begun to sink all kinds of vessels again, and President Wilson had sent the German ambassador home and recalled our ambassador to Germany. In early March, a German U-boat torpedoed our steamship the *Algonquin* without warning. Woodrow Wilson had been reelected president largely because he promised to keep us out of the European war, but folks were beginning to wonder how much more he could take from the German kaiser.

I was asleep when Dad came home; the closing of the front door must have awakened me.

"There's been another automobile accident on Dead Man's Curve," I heard him tell Mama. "Where's Noah?"

"He went to bed early," Mama said. "Was anybody hurt?"

"Two were killed," Dad said. "That makes nine who have been killed on that curve in the last two years. It should be straightened out."

"Good Lord," Mama said. "Were they anybody we knew?"

"The car was Harry Sumner's new Stutz Bearcat," Dad said. "It was going so fast it couldn't make the turn and ran off the road and hit a telephone pole, cut the pole in two pieces. The ones in the car went right through the windshield."

I had heard enough and went downstairs where Mama and Dad were sitting in the kitchen—it was warmer there.

"I thought the Sumners had gone on a trip to Bermuda," Mama said. "They usually go somewhere this time of the year."

"It wasn't them," Dad said. "It was their boy, Lester, and Clarissa Green."

I didn't cry or say anything, but I was thinking plenty, remembering how PeeWee used to ride beside Mr. Sumner in the yellow Stutz. When his father left him in the auto, PeeWee would slide over under the wheel like he had been driving it. He was a year older than me, almost fifteen, and in another year he would have been able to get a driver's license. I thought of how Mr. Sumner had taken PeeWee's pony and cart away from him and sold it to punish him for playing hooky. It wasn't hard to figure why PeeWee took his father's automobile. And remembering how Clarissa's mother had refused to let her go with the rest of us on the nature hike, I knew why she had gone with PeeWee.

"He was their only child," Mama said, "and they spoiled him so, giving him so many things most boys only dream of."

"They've been having trouble with him lately," Dad said. "Someone uptown said Harry Sumner had threatened to send him to military school where he could be taught to obey."

"And Clarissa was an only child, too," Mama said, "and from such a good family. Mary lost her husband less than a year ago in an automobile accident and now she's lost her daughter. Pretty soon it won't be safe to cross the street."

"What time did it happen, Dad?" I asked, finding my tongue.

"Lester took the car out after supper, when the servants went out for a while. Some folks saw the Stutz going up the hill by the college with its muffler wide open, about the time the Bullet blew for the mill pond crossing. It was too dark for them to see who was in the car. But they must have wondered. They found the wrecked car and the bodies on Dead Man's Curve about seven-thirty."

This curve is four miles north of our town. It is almost a right angle turn with a couple of miles of straight road where it is easy to speed on each approach to the curve.

"That poor little rich boy," Mama said, crying to herself. "Now he's dead and his parents are not even here to claim his body."

"They'll be home tomorrow night," Dad said.

Mama put a pot of coffee on the kitchen stove, but she wouldn't give me a cup. I made myself a bread and butter sandwich. Then I went upstairs to bed, but I didn't go to sleep for a long time. The town clock struck eleven and twelve and one before I slept.

When I awoke, the wren was singing and I knew it was going to be another fine spring day, but I felt strange and for a moment I thought I must be ill—then I remembered what had happened to PeeWee and Clarissa. I shivered and pulled the blankets up over my head. When Grandpappy had died, it had ended his pain, but PeeWee and Clarissa had everything ahead of them—and they came from the kind of people who had had the best of everything for a long time.

Mama had to call me to breakfast. We had buckwheat cakes, the kind that rise at night in the back of the stove, and they are a favorite of mine. But I didn't have much appetite.

"Are you all right, Noah?" Mama asked.

"Yes, ma'am," I said, but I didn't feel all right, and I was glad it was Saturday. I couldn't have made myself go to school that day—I sat right next to Clarissa.

After breakfast, I picked up yesterday's evening newspaper. President Wilson had ordered an increase in the size of our navy to 87,000 men so as to better guard our merchant ships from the German U-boats.

Mama was not used to seeing me around the house on Saturdays. She was upset, too, by what had happened to PeeWee and Clarissa. Instead of going to the meat market, she sent me.

"Get a shoulder of ham that weighs about three pounds," she said, "and be sure Mr. Carson gives you a lean one; and a pound of ground chuck; tell him to put it through the grinder twice; and a pound of lard." She gave me a list of groceries. "Stop at Mr. Leary's on the way home and pick up these things for me."

I didn't want to go anywhere until I got used to the idea of never seeing Clarissa or PeeWee anymore. I told myself that they were safe in Heaven, but that didn't make me feel much better. At the corner, I hesitated; it would have been easy to go back home. The daffodils were blooming in Miss Lizzie's flower beds. Mama always says that Miss Lizzie has the prettiest daffodils in town. Queen Street was as quiet as it always is early on a Saturday morning, before the farmers arrive to do their week's shopping.

It was a nice day with the sun warming things and the air tasting good like it always does in the early spring, after so many hours spent inside during the winter. The robins were running across the lawn of the house with all the lightening rods; that's where Mr. and Mrs. Coursey live. They bought all of the lightening rods so as to be sure they won't be struck by lightening. Now a robin was speared on one of the rods, blown there by the March gales. It was as dead as Clarissa and PeeWee, but nobody would take it down from the rod and bury it.

I started to run—I felt better running—and didn't slow down until I came to Dora Tilghman's house. She was in the front yard, loosening the soil around the crocuses and daffodils with a trowel. When she stood up, I could see from her red eyes that she had been crying.

"Isn't it terrible, Noah?" Dora said.

I nodded.

"Clarissa was my cousin," Dora said, "but sometimes we quarreled. You know how she was."

"PeeWee and Clarissa had a lot of nerve," I said. "Remember how they stayed on the Whirlpool Dip even after Ric had enough?"

"Mother says that Lester's parents gave him everything but love," Dora said. "They were too busy to give him much attention. But Mother has always been jealous of the Sumners because they have more money than we have."

While we were talking, a truck rolled along Green Street towing what was left of the Stutz Bearcat. Its front was crushed like a tin can, where it had hit the telephone pole, and all of the glass was gone from its windshield. The front wheels were also missing. Its yellow hood was streaked with something dark red—I knew what that was.

"They have to cremate their bodies, Noah," Dora said, shuddering. "The glass windshield cut them into pieces."

She started to cry and went inside her house, leaving me alone. I shivered as I watched the truck and the wreck turn the corner into Main Street.

Mickey Salmons lives next to Dora. He must have seen me and came out in his yard.

"We won't play Run, Sheep, Run, today" he said. "I feel funny—how do you feel?"

"Awful," I said, "except when I'm running—then I feel better—until I stop."

"Pop says we'll all feel better in a few days," Mickey said. "He always says that time takes care of everything. Now he's worrying about the war and thinks we'll be in it in a few days. My two brothers are old enough to go."

We walked uptown together. Mickey left me to go to the post office and I continued on to the meat market. While Mr. Carson was grinding the beef, he mentioned the accident.

"They say there's blood all over the road like somebody had stuck a pig," the butcher said as he cut the meat into small pieces with his cleaver and dropped them into the grinder. "I wouldn't have an automobile if someone offered to give me one. They're like a slaughtering house on wheels."

On the way home, I followed the back street so as not to pass Dora's house again. I didn't want to talk to her or anybody else about the accident—not for a while. I passed the garage where the Stutz had been left. A crowd of people were examining the wreck. Ric was there.

"PeeWee must have been going more than fifty miles an hour, Noah," Ric said.

"Let's not talk about it," I said.

"We all got to go sometime, and it was their time to go," Ric said. "That's what Pop says and it's good enough for me. Just think, they won't ever have to go to school anymore."

"Do you really believe it was their time?" I asked.

"Sure, the Good Lord has it all figured out and there's nothing we can do about it. When it comes our day to die, we'll die, and not before. So why worry?"

I thought about what Ric had said on my way home. It helped.

Mama met me at the gate and took one of the bags. "You

were gone a long time," she said. "I was beginning to worry about you. I don't know what I'd do if anything ever happened to you. This morning, I thanked the Good Lord that we'll never have enough to buy an automobile. There are even advantages to being poor."

"Yes, ma'am," I said, wondering if PeeWee and Clarissa had joined Grandpappy. It was only a month since he died, but it already seemed a long time ago.

"Did you hear uptown when they are going to have the funerals?" Mama asked.

"No, ma'am," I said. "Dora told me they're going to have to cremate Lester and Clarissa. They were cut to pieces by the glass in the windshield."

Mama sat down in the rocker on the front porch. "Oh, my!" she said. "I feel faint. Run and get me my smelling salts."

After she got a few sniffs of the ammonia, she felt better. "It's just as well. With the cremation, they won't need pallbearers. I was worrying about that. Since Lester sang in the children's choir and served as acolyte, you would have been asked to serve as pallbearer. It might have made you sick."

"What will they do with Clarissa, Mama?" I asked.

"Mary will take her back to the city to rest with her father."

By the time we went to church on Sunday morning, everything had been taken care of. The Sumners had returned from Bermuda, and after talking with Clarissa's mother and Reverend Hammond it was decided to have one memorial service for Clarissa and PeeWee. During the services, Reverend Hammond spoke of the accident and offered prayers for them, their parents, and friends. He has a nice voice. What he said made all of us feel better. But I still thought of what Ric said.

It was Palm Sunday, the Sunday before Easter. On the way out the church door after the services, the young rector gave each of us a small piece of palm. It was also the first of April, April Fool's Day, when we played tricks on one another, but nobody did that year in our town.

The memorial service was held the next day at 2 p.m. We were dismissed early from school—that was the second time in less than a week. Our children's choir sang the anthem we were preparing for Easter. Reverend Hammond spoke and called to Lester and Clarissa just like they could hear him.

With PeeWee gone, we had a new acolyte. Mickey Salmons was chosen to light the candles and put them out.

15

◀🐚 To Make the World Safe

After the memorial service, I went home. Dad was there, and it was only three o'clock. He and Mama were sitting in the kitchen.

"Did you hear the news uptown?" he asked.

"What news?" I asked, wondering how he could be looking for more news after what had happened.

"President Wilson has asked Congress to declare war on Germany," Dad said. "He also wants a law to draft a least half a million men into the army. The news came in over the telegraph."

I hadn't thought much about the war since the accident. "Do you think Congress will give him what he wants?" I asked.

"The way the Germans have been sinking our ships, Wilson can get almost anything he asks for," Dad said. "A few western isolationists may talk a lot, but they don't have the votes to stop him."

"They're liable to draft you, George," Mama said, "especially since you're not working steady."

"I'm forty-five," Dad said. "I'm too old to cross the ocean and fight in a foreign land."

"The way you like to play around on the river and bay, they'd put you in the navy," Mama said, winking at me.

After supper, I went up to the railroad station so as to be sure to get an evening newspaper. A lot of people had the same idea—almost half the town was there. The Bullet was half an hour late, but it had an extra supply of newspapers on board. The headline read:

WILSON ASKS CONGRESS TO DECLARE WAR ON GERMANY

I ran all the way home. The big headline scared even Mama.

"Good Lord!" she said. "I was praying it wouldn't happen again in my time. The Spanish-American War was a picnic compared to this one."

"Why didn't you fight in the Spanish-American War, Dad?" I asked.

"They didn't need many men," he said. "Those who liked to fight volunteered."

"Your father wouldn't fight to defend his own home," Mama said. "He'd turn the other cheek."

"That's the Christian thing to do," Dad said. "If everybody felt the way I do, there wouldn't ever be another war."

"If everybody felt the way you do, the Germans would come over here and conquer us," Mama said.

"The ocean is still too wide for that," Dad said.

"That evil German kaiser don't feel the way you do," Mama said. "Look how he ordered his soldiers to cut the hands off those Belgian children, just because they wouldn't salute the German flag."

"You mustn't believe everything bad you hear about the Germans," Dad said.

"You keep on talking like that and they'll put you in jail, George," Mama said, and this time she didn't wink at me.

When I went to school the next morning, everybody was talking about the president's speech.

"My brother, Colin, is going to enlist in the National Guard if Congress declares war," Ric said. "I wish I was old enough to go with him."

"I'm old enough to go," Alvin said. "I'm older than you fellows—I'll be sixteen next week."

"You have to be eighteen," Ric said.

"I'm big enough to pass for eighteen," Alvin said. "It would be a good way to get away from home. Pop was born in Germany, but I don't like the way those Germans have been cutting the hands off the Belgian children. They even torpedoed a Red Cross ship carrying nurses and supplies to help the Belgians."

"My two older brothers are going to enlist if war is declared," Mickey said.

In history class, Miss Carroll, our teacher, read President Wilson's speech to us. After she had finished, there were questions.

"What does President Wilson mean when he says the world must be made safe for democracy?" Millie asked.

"He thinks that the people of all nations should have the right to govern themselves," Miss Carroll said.

"That's a big order," Ric said. "Does he include the Chinese? There must be a billion of them."

Dora raised her hand. "We were talking about that last night," she said. "Father says it's a slogan the president has coined to help our soldiers fight better."

"What slogan did our soldiers have in the Mexican War, class?" Miss Carroll asked.

Mickey's hand was raised first. "Remember the Alamo."

I raised my hand. "And in the Spanish-American War it was 'Remember the *Maine*'."

That was Tuesday. The members of Congress debated the president's requests for the next two days. It was like Dad had said, a few congressmen and senators, largely from west of the Mississippi River, argued against a declaration of war. They repeated George Washington's warning that our country should not become entangled in foreign affairs; they said that if we entered the war, it would be a violation of the Monroe Doctrine. It insisted that European nations should keep out of the Western Hemisphere, and pledged our country to leave Europe alone. These isolationists had some good arguments. They were given their say. But on Friday, Congress passed the joint resolution declaring war on Germany. The vote in the House of Representatives was 373 to 50 in favor of the resolution. Fewer senators voted against it, and the declaration of war was sent to the president shortly after 1 p.m. We were sitting in English class when the whistle at the basket factory began to blow. The whistle at the fire department joined it, along with the church bells, and the school janitor began to ring our bell. We knew what the whistles and bells said—our country had entered the European war. It happened on Good Friday.

When I went home after school Dad was already there. He looked awfully worried.

"I wish I was a few years younger," he said. "I don't like fighting, but those Huns need a good whipping. The U.S. is going to have to do most of the job."

"Wouldn't you look pretty in a soldier suit," Mama said. "It's hard to get you to cut off the head of a chicken."

"If I was a little older, I could go," I said. "Me and Ric could go with Colin to enlist in the machine gun company at Annapolis."

"Good Lord," Mama said. "Is that where he's going?"

"A rifle ain't good enough for Colin," Dad said. "He must be planning to kill all of the Huns."

"I thank the Good Lord that neither one of you will go," Mama said.

The next day, Colin and other young men in our town went to Annapolis and joined the machine gun company of the National Guard. Its captain was a local man who had graduated from St. John's College—it was then a military college. Others enlisted in the National Guard company of infantry located here, to bring its numbers up to full strength.

When we had our Boy Scout meeting on Tuesday evening, our scoutmaster had called in Johnny Banning, one of our barbers, to help him. Johnny had fought in the Spanish-American War. While he was cutting your hair, he liked to talk about how he followed Teddy Roosevelt in his charge up San Juan Hill in Cuba. Teddy rode a horse and Johnny had to run to keep up with him.

Our scoutmaster said that while the Boy Scouts was not a military organization, we were at war, and he thought it would be a good idea for us to learn the rudiments of military drills. We could carry our staffs in place of rifles.

Johnny lined us up in patrols; each had eight men like a squad. He showed us how to come to attention and relax at ease. We learned right dress and left dress, right face and left face and about face. When we stopped, we were dizzy and facing in all directions. If Johnny had given us the order to march, our troop would have been scattered all over town.

While we were drilling, the older men stood watching us. I saw Alvin standing in the shadows. He had never joined the Boy Scouts.

When Mama heard that we had been drilling, she got mad. "They ought to know better than to try and make soldiers out of you at your age," she said.

The next day when I went to school, Ric and Alvin were both absent. At lunchtime, I walked home with Dora.

"I'm awfully worried about Ricard and Alvin," she said.

"Yesterday, Alvin was talking about running away to Baltimore and joining the Marines. It would be just like Ricard to go with him."

While I was eating lunch, Ric's older sister, Annie, came looking for him. He had started to school that morning but hadn't come home at noon.

"Ric wasn't in school this morning, Annie," I said. "Alvin Bonner was absent, too."

"Those two have been as thick as thieves the last few days," Annie said. "Just before I came over here, Mama discovered that Ricard had taken most of his clothes from his room. He must have sneaked them out during the night when the rest of us were asleep."

"Alvin told Dora yesterday that he was going to run off to Baltimore and join the Marines," I said.

"That's where they both have gone," Annie said, and went home.

Those first days after we entered the war were exciting ones. The older men of our town, even Dad, met and organized a Home Guard to defend us in case the Germans should come up the Chesapeake Bay in one of their submarines. Earlier in the war, the German commercial sub, the *Deutschland*, had docked in Baltimore with a cargo of dyes and chemicals. The Home Guard began to drill once a week, just like the Boy Scouts, on the town square.

Even the women changed because of the war. Some joined the Red Cross and prepared to go overseas with our soldiers. Others went to the city to work in the war industries. Several of our younger women went to Clifton's Barber shop and had their long hair cut off. Ric's father said if Annie had her hair bobbed like a show girl, she needn't come home because he wouldn't let her in. She had her hair cut anyway—Mr. Lawrence had to change his mind.

But he wouldn't go after Ric and said if a son of his didn't have any better sense than to run away from a good home and join the Marines, he could go. Mr. Bonner must have felt the same way about Alvin. Since he was born in Germany, he had to be careful what he said or did. The few people in our town who had relatives in Germany kept very quiet—they were closely watched. There was talk of German spies who might poison us. The town's water supply was guarded twenty-four hours a day.

Toward the end of May, the ones who had enlisted when war was declared began to come home for furloughs. Colin was wearing corporal stripes and a big grin when he came to see us. After several weeks in a training camp in Alabama, he looked better than we had ever seen him.

"When are they going to ship you overseas, Colin?" Dad asked.

"I don't know, Mr. George," Colin said, "and if I did, I couldn't tell you. We'll have more training in France before going into the trenches."

"Ain't you afraid, Colin?" Mama asked.

"Not when I think why we are fighting this war," he said. "We are going to make the world safe for democracy."

Ric and Alvin came home on leave the last week of school, wearing their Marine uniforms, looking almost like men. They walked down Main Street, in step, singing a song that always ended, "Hinky, dinky, Parley Vou." It had a lot of verses and some of them had dirty words, but nobody bothered them. Except the girls, the girls really did go for the uniforms.

"Hi, there, kid," Ric said when he saw me. He had never called me kid before.

"When are you going to France, Ric?" I asked.

"Pretty soon," he said, "and it can't be too soon for us. Me and Alvin can't wait to meet those French girls!"

"Ain't you afraid of being killed?" I asked.

"It's not in the cards for me, kid," he said. "I feel just like Colin. The Germans will never make the bullet with my name on it."

16

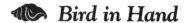 *Bird in Hand*

I was smoking a cigarette in the woodshed. Mama must have known what I was doing, but she never said anything as long as I kept the cigarettes out of the house. Most of the boys in our town started smoking early. It was easy to buy cigarettes. Dad used to send me uptown to buy a pack of Sweet Caporals or Little Recruits for him. The law said you had to be eighteen to buy tobacco, but nobody thought it was wrong to buy cigarettes for your father or older brother. After a while you stopped telling the storekeeper the tobacco was for your father and he didn't ask.

The first cigarette I smoked made me as sick as a dog, and I never really got interested in smoking until the WCTU in our town had a campaign in the public schools trying to get all of us to take a pledge never to drink alcohol or use tobacco in any of its noxious forms. The lady who led this temperance crusade must have weighed two hundred pounds. She had to eat about five meals a day to weigh that much, but she lectured us on how to live a temperate life. Many of us boys wouldn't sign the pledge and began to smoke after the crusade ended.

Mama got Doctor Salmons to talk to me about smoking. He told me that it would stunt my growth, but he was six feet tall and he smoked a pack of cigarettes a day. Batty Benson, who started school with me but dropped out in the third grade, had been smoking years before the rest of us and he was six feet four. I guess he would have become a giant if he had taken that WCTU pledge and never touched the weed.

Anyway, I was smoking in the woodshed when I heard the kitchen door open and close and Dad's voice. Mama must have been waiting for him. She flew right in to him.

"You've got to get a steady job, George," she said. "With the war going on, a dollar don't buy half as much as it did. And you know I don't do much sewing during the summer."

"Me and Jesse are going crabbing as soon as it gets warmer," Dad said. "The crabs are late coming up the river this year."

"Crabbing," Mama said. "I call it progging. Most days you come home empty handed. I want you to bring home a pay envelope every Saturday. A bird in the hand is worth two in the bush."

"We ain't never starved," Dad said.

"That's not your fault," Mama said. "And it ain't patriotic not to be working when a war is going on. The next thing you know, they will be putting you into the army. Then where would you be?"

"I'm too old for that," Dad said.

"You're only forty-five," Mama said. "If the war goes on long enough they're liable to draft you."

"Do you really think they might put one of those soldier suits on me?" Dad asked, and I could tell he was getting worried.

"You've got two arms and two legs," Mama said.

"Maybe I ought to go to Baltimore and get a job in the shipyard," Dad said. "They can't draft you if you work in a shipyard."

"The basket factory is a lot closer," Mama said. "You wouldn't go to the city by yourself, anyway. You know how the city scares you."

"Me and Jesse might go together," Dad said. "Jim Cable is making fifty dollars a week as a carpenter in Baltimore. If he can do it, so can me and Jesse."

"You're no carpenter," Mama said. "I can't get you to lift a hammer around the house."

"Neither is Jim. They say anybody who can drive a nail can get a job."

"Would you send me a part of your pay every Saturday?" Mama asked. "We might save enough money to send Noah to the preparatory school at the college. Some of the teachers at the public school let the boys run wild."

"It's expensive living in the city," Dad said, "But I ought to be able to send you half of what I make."

"Provided you don't lose it gambling," Mama said.

"I ain't gambling in the city," Dad said. "Them city card sharpers are too slick for me."

"That's what you say, now," Mama said.

"It would be nice to have Noah go to the preparatory school with the Brewster boys," Dad said.

"He's smarter than any of them," Mama said. "He ought to have a chance."

"I want him to have a better chance than I had," Dad said. "If Jesse will go with me, I'll really get a job in Baltimore. I'm too old to wear a soldier suit."

"You go and talk to Jesse right away, before you change your mind," Mama said.

I heard the front door shut and Dad whistling as he walked along the oyster shell road. Mama started to hum a tune.

I was in the kitchen when Dad came back, excited, and talking a blue streak. He usually didn't say much unless he had a couple of drinks.

"Jesse says he will go with me," he said. "Where's my hatchet and saw, Noah?"

"You're not going this minute, are you?" Mama asked.

"No, but I want to sharpen them," Dad said.

I found Dad's tools in the woodshed. They were rusty—it took him most of the afternoon to make them look like anything. It was almost four o'clock when Mr. Jesse came in.

"How do they look, Jesse?" Dad asked, holding up the tools.

"They'll pass," Mr. Jesse said. "We ought to buy some carpenter's overalls and pencils, George. They would make us look like real carpenters. Have you looked at the ads of the morning *Sun* for jobs?"

"It ain't pleasant reading," Mr. Jesse said. "Look under C for carpenters."

Dad ran his finger down the columns. "Here's carpenters to build residences," he said.

"We couldn't do that," Mr. Jesse said. "It takes a real carpenter to build a residence. Don't none of the shipyards have an ad for carpenters?"

"I don't see none," Dad said.

Mama was listening. "What's the matter with you two?" she said. "I was afraid it was too good to be true. Now you've got cold feet before you even start to work."

She looked over Dad's shoulder. "There's an ad for carpenters at Fort Meade, building barracks for soldiers. You ought to be able to do that."

"I never built a barrack," Dad said. "Have you, Jesse?"

"They're like a big chicken house," Mr. Jesse said. "We could do that."

Mama put her finger on the ad. "Carpenters at Fort Meade,"

she read. "Rough work. $1.25 an hour for an eight-hour day, time and a half for overtime."

"They might get us mixed up with the rest of the soldiers and march us away," Dad said.

"Not as long as you keep working," Mama said.

Mr. Jesse was figuring in his head. "If we worked ten hours a day, six days a week, how much would we get in that pay envelope on Saturday? How much would we make, Noah?"

That was easy: "forty hours at $1.25 an hour would be $50.00; eight hours at $1.25 would be $10.00 for a total of $60.00 for their regular work. For the overtime, twelve hours at $1.25 would be $15.00 times 1½ would be $22.50. Add the two together and you get $82.50."

"Good Lord," Dad said. "Did you calculate that right?" He figured it in his head. "That's right," he said, "more than eighty dollars a week. How long do you reckon that work will last?"

"At that rate, it won't have to last long," Mr. Jesse said.

"When are you going?" Mama asked.

"What say we leave on the *B. S. Ford,* tomorrow, Jesse?" Dad said. "That will give us time to be there to get the jobs early Monday morning."

"That's all right with me," Mr. Jesse said, "but we'll have to have enough money to feed and bed us until our first pay day."

"I can let you have ten dollars, George," Mama said. "I was saving it for a new stove, but you'll need it now."

"I've got ten dollars at home," Mr. Jesse said. "Let's go uptown and buy those carpenter's overalls and pencils."

"Don't you spend any more money than you have to," Mama said, as they went out the door.

"There goes a pair," she said to me. "I hope they don't meet anybody uptown who is drinking."

"Maybe they'll get into a poker game," I said.

"You are certainly getting pessimistic, Noah," Mama said. "I don't know where you get it from."

Dan and Mr. Jesse were back in less than an hour. Mama shortened the pants of the overalls for them.

"These denims look so new," Mama said. "Anybody would know you're not experienced carpenters."

"Maybe if we put them on and wear them, they'll look older," Dad said. So they put them on.

The next morning, I got up early to see Dad and Mr. Jesse off. Dad had a big breakfast and Mama packed him a lunch in a shoe box.

"Maybe you'd better pin your money in your pocket with a safety pin, George," she said.

"You talk like I wasn't any older than Noah," he said.

Mama sighed. "You do seem awfully young in some ways, George."

Dad finished his breakfast and picked up his hatchet and saw. He was ready to go.

"Ain't you going to kiss me good-bye, George?" Mama said, and there was a tear in her eye.

"I knew there was something I forgot," Dad said and kissed her.

"You write to me, George, and tell us what happens," Mama said.

"Let me carry your suitcase to the wharf, Dad," I said.

When I went out the door, I looked back. Mama was really crying. Dad was glad to have me for company walking to the wharf.

"Do you think you could scrape the bateau and get her ready to paint, Noah?" he asked. "All I did this spring was to give her bottom a coat of red lead—money has been that tight. I may be able to get home for a weekend soon and we could paint her."

"Sure, Dad," I said.

We were still a block from the wharf when the *B. S. Ford* blew a long blast.

Dad started to run and I tried to keep up with him, but the suitcase was getting heavier. We reached the wharf after the deckhands had pulled the gangplank aboard and were taking in the mooring lines. We could see Mr. Jesse on the second deck.

"I'll have to get my ticket on board," Dad said, and jumped on to the *Ford*. I tossed him his suitcase and tools. The steamboat blew again as she backed out into the river. Dad and Mr. Jesse waved.

Mama wouldn't let me leave home after it got dark. She was sort of scared, knowing Dad had gone away.

"I hope nothing happens to him," she said.

"Dad is lucky," I said. "Nothing will happen to him—nothing ever does."

The next morning, while I was getting ready to go to the cove, she started to stew again.

"You be sure to stop at the post office for the mail at noon, Noah," she said. "Your father may have dropped me a postcard to let us know he arrived safely."

"Yes, ma'am," I said, but there wasn't any card from Dad. I went again, after the evening train came in—still there wasn't any word from him.

"No news is good news," Mama said, rocking to quiet her nerves.

Tuesday noon, when I stopped at the post office, the clerk said Mama had already been there. When I got home she was sitting on the front porch fanning herself.

"Did you hear from Dad?" I asked.

"He sent me this postcard, written right out where everybody can read it," she said. "Look," and she gave me the card.

"Dear Evelyn," it read, "Arrived safely and am working at Camp Meade tomorrow. Me and Jesse lost almost all our money on the boat playing poker, but we will get an advance on our wages. Love to you and Noah—George." There was an address on Hanover Street.

"Everybody in town will know he lost his money playing poker," Mama said.

"Anyway, he didn't have much to lose," I said.

"And he would pick somewhere in South Baltimore to stay," Mama said. "It's not respectable down by the wharves."

A week later Mama received a letter from Dad with a money order for twenty-five dollars. She sent me to the post office to cash it.

"I can't tell you how this makes me feel, Noah," she said. "Having something in reserve makes all the difference. A bird in the hand is worth two in the bush."

"What did Dad say in the letter?" I asked.

"He's coming home to see us next Saturday, on the train; the *B. S. Ford* leaves before he finishes work."

"I didn't know Dad liked to travel on trains," I said.

"He won't have a chance to gamble like he would on the steamboat," Mama said. "Jesse is coming with him."

"I'd better get the bateau ready," I said. "We might paint it Sunday."

"Remember the Sabbath and keep it holy," Mama said.

"Sunday is the only time Dad can work on his boat, Mama," I said. "Don't you think the Lord will know Dad has a steady job and is sending money home?"

Mama didn't answer my question. "Don't you cut yourself working on that old boat," she said.

Almost every day, I went down to the cove and worked on the bateau. I used one of Mama's old case knives to scrape the paint off the decks and sides, sharpening it with a file. While I was working, I watched the old heron fishing in the shallows off the point. He would stand in the same place for five minutes, long beak ready to spear any minnow that might come in his range. Then he would walk slowly along, lifting his feet like an old waterman wading along a muddy bottom. Or all of a sudden he would start to mutter and cough like he had swallowed a minnow the wrong way. Then he would take off and pitch in a tree, still muttering to himself.

I felt good, scraping the boat in the sun. Schools of small fish, menhaden, were swimming across the cove, followed by larger fish that fed on them. When a rockfish struck the minnows, they scattered in all directions, jumping from the water like silver splinters. I don't like to see the big fish eat the little fish, but Dad says that's the way life is.

I wondered what Dad was doing and wishing he was with me. A river man would rather paint his boat than do most anything. On Friday, the bateau was ready to paint. I did cut myself on a piece of broken glass I used to scrape the stern, but I didn't tell Mama.

Saturday was a long day for both Mama and me. The evening train didn't arrive until after seven o'clock. We decided to meet Dad at the station. Along about four o'clock Mama dressed in her Sunday best, but I wore my regular clothes. Mama kept watching the clock and wouldn't let me leave the house.

"You might wander off where you can't hear me call," she said, so I sat down and watched her getting supper. She even had meat cakes made out of round steak instead of chuck. But we couldn't eat without Dad, so she put all the food in the oven to keep warm.

At six-thirty, we left for the station. "Our clock might be slow," Mama said.

When we got to the station, nobody was there but Simon, the colored man who drives the hack for the hotel.

"Hello, Simon," I said, "is the train on time?"

"That's what the station agent says," he replied. "You folks expecting someone?"

"My father is coming home," I said, "He's working in Baltimore."

Mama called to me and whispered, "You mustn't talk to colored people, not even respectable ones like Simon."

Just then the Bullet blew for the mill pond crossing. "Here she comes, Mama," I said. "Do you think Dad brought us any presents?"

We could see her smoke. Click, click, click, her wheels sounded on the track; then the engineer put on her brakes, and the hissing white steam escaped into the air. The locomotive was pulling two passenger cars, one for white people and one for the colored.

The conductor stepped off before the train stopped and the passengers followed. There were a couple of drummers wearing derby hats with big cases of samples and five or six other people but I didn't see Dad or Mr. Jesse.

"They must not have come," Mama said. "Something must have happened to them."

"Maybe they had to work," I said, turning away from the station.

"Where are 'mongst you going?" a voice called, and it was Dad. He was all dressed up in a new suit with a silk shirt and straw hat; he had even started to grow a mustache. Mr. Jesse looked different, too.

"Good Lord," Mama said, "we didn't know you. You look just like a city man."

"We've been getting around, eh, Jesse?" Dad said, winking. When he kissed me, his mustache was prickly.

As we walked toward home, Dad even walked differently, like he was going some place.

"You've lost some weight, George," Mama said. "Ain't you getting enough to eat?"

"It comes from working hard and sweating," Dad said. "I've pulled in my belt a couple of inches, but I feel fine."

"I've got your bateau ready to paint, Dad," I said.

"That's good," he said. "We'll paint it as soon as the dew dries tomorrow morning, if your good mother doesn't mind me breaking the Sabbath."

"Anything you do is all right with me, George," Mama said. I'd never seen her so meek.

When we got home, we sat on the porch while Mama put supper on the table.

"I want you to go up to the hardware store after supper, Noah," Dad said. "Get a half gallon of white for the topsides and a quart of gray enamel for the deck. Better get a new paint brush and a quart of turpentine, too."

He took a big roll of bills out of his pocket and peeled off five dollars.

Mama had a good supper. Besides the meat cakes, we had fresh peas, mashed potatoes, and a custard for desert. While we were eating Mama questioned Dad.

"Don't ask me anything until I get some good food into me," Dad said. "There's nothing like home cooking. Let's move to Baltimore so I can be well fed every day."

"About the time we got settled, you might lose your job," Mama said. "Then where would we be?"

"I've already lost my job," Dad said.

"I might have known," was all Mama could say.

"But I've got another one," Dad said. "Next Sunday I go to work as a rigger on a crane for the Maryland Shipbuilding Company. We finished the last of the barracks today, but our foreman is going to take me and Jesse to the shipyard with him."

"Will it pay as much?" Mama asked.

"It'll pay more, $1.50 an hour," Dad said, "and at the speed they are building the wooden ships, there will be work for a year or more or until the war ends."

"We're not so young," Mama said. "It would be hard for me to leave my friends and the church. The city is so big and strange."

"I talked it over with Carrie and she said she would board with us if we move to Baltimore," Dad said. Aunt Carrie lives in Baltimore where she works as a bookkeeper for a lumber company.

"That would help," Mama said, "but it must be hard to rent a house in the city with a war going on."

"We could find one if we are not too particular," Dad said.

"I'd like to have a house with pretty white marble steps and a tile entrance with a bathroom," Mama said.

"I don't know whether we could get all that," Dad said, "but we could try."

"We don't want to jump too quick, George," Mama said. "Let's wait another month and see how much money we have."

"That's another thing," Dad said. "Noah could make five dollars a day carrying water in the shipyard. How about that, son?"

"He's too young to work in a shipyard," Mama said. "He won't be fourteen until next month."

"He could pass for sixteen," Dad said. "That's the age they have to be."

"We'll wait awhile and see how things go," Mama said.

The next morning after breakfast me and Dad went down to the cove.

"What will you do with the bateau if we move to the city, Dad?" I asked.

"Sell her or give her away. Maybe I'll give her to Lawrence Duer. He helped me put in a new plank a couple of years ago."

"Don't give her away too soon, Dad," I said. "We might come back again."

"You've done a nice job of scraping her, son," he said. "We'll start from the top and work down."

I opened the deck paint and stirred it while Dad cleaned one of our old brushes. We went to work, Dad whistling, and stopping once in a while to look across the cove.

"How are the soft crabs shedding, Noah?" he asked.

"There's not many sloughs," I said.

"I sure would like to have a couple of soft crabs fried in butter," he said. "You can buy them in the city, but I like to eat them when they've just backed out of their hard shell."

"We might catch a couple of peelers and go fishing under the bridge this afternoon," I said.

Dad watched the tide wetting a stake. "She's falling off, now," he said. "It'll be just right about four o'clock this afternoon." Then he remembered. "The train leaves at three o'clock," he said, sighing. "I've been feeling good, Noah, making real money and sending part of it home, but when I see my bateau and the river, I know it ain't right. I'll pay for it—everything has a price—and in the end I'll wish we'd never left the river."

"You can make a lot of money and then we'll come back and buy a place right on the river, Dad," I said.

"Maybe that's the answer," he said.

"I'll help, I'll get a job as a water boy," I said.

"But we'll come back to the river, don't forget that," Dad said.

17

Water Boy

The next time Dad came home from the city he didn't even tell us he was coming. Mama had cleared the supper dishes off the table when I heard the front gate click and there he was, looking more than ever like a city man. He was carrying his coat under his arm, and that gave us a better chance to see the lavender silk shirt he was wearing. His mustache was thicker.

"Hello," he said. "Am I in time for supper?"

"Supper is over but the stores are open on Saturday night," Mama said. "Noah, go up to the meat market and get a pound of round steak. Tell Mr. Carson to put it through the grinder twice."

Dad peeled a dollar bill off his roll and gave it to me.

When I got back, he was on his second cup of coffee.

"The way things are going, I'll have work at the shipyard for another year, anyway," he said. "Last week with my double time, I made more than a hundred dollars."

"What's double time, Dad?" I asked.

"If I work Saturday afternoons and Sundays, I get double my hourly pay. Last Sunday, I made thirty dollars."

"That's a lot of money to make in one day," Mama said, "even if it was on a Sunday."

"Better the day, better the deed," Dad said. "Besides, it's patriotic."

Mama kept talking while she was making the meat cakes. She adds a few stale bread crumbs to make them go farther. Then she cooks them real slow in an iron skillet. They taste great.

"When are we going to move to Baltimore, Mother?" Dad asked.

"That's up to you, George," she said.

"I've got a job and I'm keeping it," he said. "My stomach is getting tired of restaurant grub."

"We don't have enough money to move," Mama said. "I've saved a hundred dollars, but by the time we paid for moving the furniture and the first month's rent, there wouldn't be anything left. If anything happened to you, where would we be?"

"Nothing ever happens to me," Dad said. "How much money would you need to move to the city?"

"We could do it with three hundred dollars."

"And you have one hundred," Dad said, taking out his roll and slipping some dollar bills off the top. Underneath, I could see yellow flashing, and he dropped two strange looking bills on the kitchen table. "There you are."

Mama sat down quick. "Hundred dollar bills," she said. "How did you get the money, George? You couldn't earn that much."

"Call it a lucky investment," Dad said.

"You've been gambling again."

"And I won," he said. "What's wrong with that? The farmer gambles every day with the weather—I only gamble once in a while. Don't you want it?"

"I'll take it," Mama said, and went upstairs with the two bills. We could hear her opening and closing drawers, looking for a good place to hide the money. Then she came downstairs again.

"I only hope I don't forget where I hid that money," she said.

"Where did you hide it?" Dad asked.

"Where you can't find it and gamble it away. How much more did you win?"

"Don't you worry about that," he said, slapping his pants pocket.

"You'd better give it to me so you won't lose it," Mama said.

"You won't get your hands on this roll," Dad said, "and to save you the trouble of looking through my pants pockets, I'll sleep with it under my pillow."

Mama saw she couldn't get Dad's money and started washing the dishes.

"How are the crabs running, Noah?" Dad asked.

"They're late coming up the river," I said.

"Everything is mixed up," he said. "It must be the war."

"He's underfoot in the house half the time," Mama said. "Noah ought to get a job somewhere, too."

"I'm glad you brought that up, Evaline," Dad said. "I asked my foreman in the shipyard again about a job for Noah. He can make five dollars a day carrying water for the men. I'd like to take him back with me tomorrow."

"That would leave me all alone," Mama said. "I don't know whether I could stand it alone."

"It would only be until we find a house in the city," Dad said. "The manager at the boarding house says he can put a cot in my room for Noah."

"That's another thing," Mama said. "Is it clean where you are staying? I don't want Noah getting some terrible disease in the city."

"It's not as clean as you keep a house, but it's clean enough."

"How's the food? You know Noah has a weak stomach."

"It ain't like home cooking, but Noah can stand it until we move. That oughten to be more than a couple of weeks."

"With all the money you got in your pocket, I don't see why you want Noah working," Mama said.

"I get awfully lonely," Dad said. "Some days I feel like quitting and coming home. And I'm liable to do it."

"All right," she said, "I'll let Noah go with you, if he wants to go. You've been talking so big and flashing all that money, I didn't know you were lonely for us."

"Do you want to go with me and work in the shipyard, son?" Dad asked.

"If you can stand it, I can," I said.

"Your mother can get your clothes ready for you," Dad said.

"Things are happening so fast," Mama said. "I'm going to have indigestion if I don't slow up. Noah will be sick with an upset stomach if he's not careful."

"There's nothing wrong with his stomach," Dad said. "Anybody who can eat raw oysters like he does, at his age, don't have to fear for their stomach. I couldn't look a raw oyster in the eye until I was past eighteen."

"Noah can use my suitcase," Mama said. "I'll get his things packed tonight, so there won't be a hurry tomorrow."

Sunday morning I went to church with Mama.

"Your father won't be taking you to church in the city," she said, while we were having our Sunday dinner.

"I'm going to take him to the Gayety Theater, Evaline," Dad said.

"Noah is too young to go to the Gayety, George," Mama said.

"What's the Gayety?" I asked.

"It's something like the hoochy-koochy girls at the county fair, only better," Dad said.

"You mean worse," Mama said. "The Gayety is a burlesque theater, Noah."

"What's burlesque?" I asked.

"That's a show where the orchestra plays and the women take off most of their clothes," she said. "You are not old enough to see that."

"Have you ever been to a burlesque show, Evaline?" Dad asked.

"You know I wouldn't put my foot inside that kind of a show," Mama said.

"Then how can you tell Noah what it is like?" he asked. "The Gayety has good comedians, like Sliding Billy Watson, and I want Noah to see them."

"I'm sure you go to see the comedians," Mama said, but she didn't say I couldn't go. When you are old enough to work steady, you can do most anything.

"You've always been such a good boy, Noah," she said. "Don't let any of those bad city boys get you into trouble."

"I won't," I said.

"And stick close to your father. He needs you to help him as much as you need him."

"Yes, ma'am," I said.

I'd never been to Baltimore on the train before. Mama always went to Baltimore on the *B. S. Ford* to do her shopping. It was exciting getting on the train with Dad. Mama didn't go to the station with us. She was afraid she might cry when we both left her; she didn't like going home to an empty house.

My stomach felt funny when the train started, but I soon got used to it and listened to the clicking of the wheels on the track as I watched the country flash by the window. It was exciting when the train crossed the Susquehanna River on a high bridge. It was almost dark when we pulled into Union Station in Baltimore.

"You'll have to learn your way about in the city, Noah," Dad said, "and if you ever get lost, any policeman will put you straight."

"I'm not planning to go anywhere by myself for a while, Dad," I said.

"We might get separated in a crowd," he said. "The city is so crowded with all the soldiers and war workers."

"How do we get to the boarding house, Dad?" I asked. "I'm almost starved."

"That's on Hanover Street," he said. "The No. 2 streetcar goes right past the door. But the No. 2 doesn't run by this railroad station, so we'll get a streetcar that will connect with the No. 2. Is that plain?"

"I guess so," I said, and we boarded a streetcar with No. 19 on the front.

"I want two transfers to the No. 2 car going south," Dad said to the conductor. "Where do I get it?"

"North Avenue and Charles Street," the conductor said, and gave Dad a couple of slips of paper.

"It's that easy," Dad said, pleased with himself.

"How do we know when we get to North Avenue and Charles?" I asked, looking out the window. It was dark outside.

"I think we are on North Avenue now," Dad said. "The conductor will call out the streets."

I listened but the conductor jumbled his words. "Foolton," he growled. "Foolton next."

"St. Paul is the street before Charles," Dad said.

"Maybe we passed Charles," I said.

"I'll ask the conductor," Dad said. I watched the man nod "no" and hold up three fingers that meant we had three more blocks before transferring to the No. 2.

When the conductor called, "Charles," we got off.

"I never feel right until I get on old No. 2," Dad said. "It will take us to grub and a bed."

Pretty soon one came clanging along with No. 2 on the front. Ten minutes later we were standing in front of the boarding house.

"The dining room is in the basement," Dad said, leading the way down the steps. When he opened the door, I smelled something that sort of turned my stomach. It was a mixture of stale air, tobacco smoke, whiskey, and urine.

The room was small and smoky with three tables, chairs, and a counter with a cash register and a box of cigars. Two men were playing dominoes at one of the tables, and a man wearing a green eyeshade was sitting on a stool behind the counter.

"Hi, Frank," Dad said to the man on the stool. "Where's Jesse? This is my boy, Noah."

"Jesse wasn't feeling good and decided to go home," Frank said. "I'll have a cot put in your room for the boy. Do you want something to eat?"

"We're almost starved," Dad said. "What do you have that's good?"

"The veal cutlet ain't bad," Frank said.

"Do you like veal cutlets, Noah?" Dad asked.

"I guess so," I said, but by this time I had lost most of my appetite. Everything was so greasy, even the people, and I didn't like the sound of the sizzling gas light—it was like a firecracker about to explode.

We sat down at a table with a greasy red tablecloth, and Frank walked through a swinging door into the kitchen. We waited a long time before a woman with a dirty towel tied around her waist brought us two plates with the veal cutlets and vegetables.

"Does the boy drink coffee?" she asked Dad.

"I'd rather have milk," I said.

"We don't have no milk," she said. "Do you want coffee?"

"O.K.," I said.

The food was greasy, too, but I was still hungry enough to eat it and drink a large cup of strong coffee.

"Would you like to take a walk, Noah?" Dad asked after we had finished.

"I'd just like to go to bed," I said. "Tomorrow is going to be a big day, and my stomach is sort of excited."

"You're not going to get sick on me, are you?" Dad asked.

"No, Dad," I said. "I'll be all right tomorrow."

We carried our suitcases to his room on the third floor. I didn't realize how warm it was until we climbed the stairs. The room was just under a tin roof.

"Whew," Dad said, and opened all the windows. They didn't have any screens and the night bugs began to fly in and hit the walls close to the gas light. But there was a cot against the wall for me to sleep on, and I was ready to use it.

"Let's get undressed and turn out the light," Dad said. "Then the night bugs will fly somewhere else."

We did.

"Always be sure to turn the gas off and don't blow it out like you would our coal oil lamp at home, Noah," Dad said, as he turned out the light.

I stretched out on the cot and was almost asleep when I felt something crawling on me. "Maybe it's one of the night bugs,"

I thought, reaching for it. Before I could find the bug, it bit me, and I knew it wasn't a mosquito.

"Something bit me, Dad," I called, "something big."

He must have been almost asleep, too, but he got up and lit the light. Five big black bugs jumped off my cot and disappeared into a hole in the wall.

"They're only bed bugs," Dad said. "If they bother you again, slap them—that will scare them off."

Every time I dozed off, those same bed bugs came out of their hole and bit me. When I lighted the gas, the night bugs came flying in the windows. Dad was fast asleep and didn't even hear me. Finally, I moved the cot out into the middle of the room and that fooled the bugs. They couldn't find me, so I went to sleep.

The next morning we were up at light and had a breakfast of ham and eggs before starting for the shipyard. It took an hour and a half to get there, so we left the boarding house at five-thirty. I liked the city better early in the morning; it was quieter and the only folks in a hurry were the milkmen. Everybody else was still half asleep. We had to pay the conductor four different times before coming to the shipyard. It had a high fence around it with barbed wire on the top, just like Miss Lizzie's fence to her chicken yard, but a lot higher. The employment office was outside the fence. That was where we went.

"I've brought my boy to get a job carrying water," Dad said. "Mr. Scott, the rigger foreman, told me he would speak to you."

The man at the window looked around and said something to another man at a desk. Then he turned and spoke to Dad.

"Are you working on a crane?"

"Yes, sir," Dad said, showing the man his badge and number.

"All right," the manager said, "but that boy of yours doesn't look very old."

"He was sixteen last month," Dad said.

The manager took my name and gave me a badge like Dad's to pin on. "You'll need this to get through the gate," he said. "Report to the foreman of the water boys at the well." He pointed to where a group of boys were standing with buckets. "You'll get sixty cents an hour plus your carfare to and from the city."

"I've got to leave you now, Noah," Dad said, "but I'll see you at the restaurant at noon."

He walked off toward the gates and I moved to the well. "I'm the new water boy," I said to a man who was giving out the buckets.

"The new one," he said. "You and ten others are new today. Seems like we can't keep a water boy more than a week." He gave me a bucket and a dipper.

"Now, listen, you guys," he said to us. "You fill your buckets here and carry the water to the men inside the yard. One boy to a gang of men, and no sleeping under the lumber piles. If you loaf, I'll know and fire you right away."

I filled my bucket and walked toward the gate beside a redheaded boy who was about my size.

"Are you new?" he asked me.

"Yes," I said.

"Me, too. What's your name?"

"Noah."

"What a name to pin on a guy," he said. "It's almost as bad as mine, Gerald, but everybody calls me 'Reds'."

"How far do you think it is to the workers?" I asked.

"One of the old guys said it's a mile," he said. "This bucket is getting heavy. Let's put them down awhile."

"Maybe our foreman is watching," I said.

"He just saw us through the gate," Reds said. "Most of the other fellows are resting."

We put our buckets on the ground and I picked up a stone and threw it into the marsh and doggone if it didn't flush a shitepoke. That made me feel a lot better.

"The faster we water them, the faster we have to carry another bucket from the well," one of the older fellows said.

"How many buckets do you carry a day?" Reds asked.

"That all depends who you are," this older guy said. "New boys have to carry more than us older fellows, at least for a week."

"Who says so?" Reds demanded.

"I say so," the older guy said. "There's more of us older fellows. If you don't do what we say, we'll beat your heads in."

"You just try it," Reds said.

"Here comes the foreman," somebody yelled, and we all picked up our buckets and moved on toward the ships. I came to a gang of men moving lumber and one of them called for water, so I put the bucket down. There were white men and black men working together and they didn't mind drinking out of the same dipper.

After the way the older fellow talked, I decided to work by myself. That morning I carried five buckets of water, and by noon I was ready to rest and eat something. There was a large building near the three ships marked "Restaurant" and that's where I found Dad. He had already bought me a lunch so we found a shady spot in the shadow of one of the ships.

"This is the one I'm working on," Dad said, pointing to the huge crane beside it. "I help feed the crane."

"What does it do?" I asked.

"It lifts the ship timbers in place. Every part of the frame has to be cut out separately and bolted on. Over at Sparrow's Point, they're making vessels of steel and launching one every two weeks. The war is liable to be over before we finish the first of these wooden boats. How do you like your job, boy?"

"It'll be all right when I get used to it, Dad."

"Take it easy, that's what everybody else is doing," he said. "Don't try to water all the men yourself."

The whistle blew sending us back to work.

It got hotter in the afternoon with the men shouting "water boy" all the time, but there weren't many of the boys around. The two or three of us who were there kept running until our tongues were hanging out. On the way back to the well, I met Reds.

"Where have you been all day, Noah?" he asked. "Sleeping under a lumber pile?"

"I've been working hard," I said. "I've carried eight buckets of water since morning."

"You trying to kid somebody?" he asked. "You must have walked twenty-five miles carrying that load. You want to kill yourself?"

When the quitting whistle blew, I met Dad outside the gate. It seemed like I had been working for a month instead of a day. I slept most of the way back to the city. Every time the conductor collected a fare, I would open my eyes, then I would go back to sleep again. Dad shook me when we came to the transfer street, and I stayed awake until we reached the boarding house.

"You'll feel better when you get some food and a cup of coffee inside you," Dad said.

"I don't want any supper," I said. "All I want is to go to bed."

"You've got to eat something," he said, and took me down to the dining room. He was right about the coffee. It did pep me up.

"How'd you like to go to a movie?" Dad asked. "We could

see *The Perils of Pauline* or a cowboy picture." Dad seldom went to the movies.

"All right," I said, so we walked over to Baltimore Street, where there was a string of movie theaters. We looked at the signs and picked one that had Pearl White and two cowboy pictures, one with William S. Hart. I went to sleep before the last picture was over and Dad awoke me when it was time to leave.

The bugs didn't bother me that night. I didn't even dream. I just slept.

18

☙ Moving to Baltimore

That night after supper, we met Aunt Carrie in front of the Sun Building and looked at the "for rent" ads that were posted on a bulletin board. They would be in the newspaper the next morning, but by going to the Sun Building, we could see them earlier.

Aunt Carrie was glad to see us. She's lived in the city since she was a young girl. She must have been lonely, but she never complained. After reading the ads, Aunt Carrie took several addresses down and we boarded a streetcar. She has lived so long in the city that she can go anywhere without asking a policeman.

When we reached the first address, somebody had beat us to it and rented the house. The same thing happened with the second address.

"We're just wasting streetcar fare, Carrie," Dad said.

"I only have one more address," she said. "Let's try it."

The house was in East Baltimore near Clifton Park. Only when we got there, it was also close to one of the city dumps. I'm not especially against dumps, but Aunt Carrie didn't like it. Dad was tired and wanted to get the thing settled.

"It's not prize," he said, "but it is vacant and the roof doesn't leak. We'd better pay the first month's rent before someone else gets it."

"I don't believe I could stand the smell of that dump," Aunt Carrie said.

"We'll only get it when the wind is from the east," Dad said. "The wind is mostly from the south in the summer, leastwise it is on the river."

"It's such a dirty neighborhood," Aunt Carrie said.

"There won't be much dirt in the house after Evaline gets here," Dad said.

"Well, if you think you can be happy here, I'll try it," Aunt Carrie said.

"If we find a better place, we can move," Dad said.

"We'd better find the agent who collects the rent and pay him right away," Aunt Carrie said.

We boarded another streetcar that carried us to a tall office building. Only a few of its windows were lighted.

"Won't his office be closed this time of night?" Dad asked.

"There's a chance he might be there," Aunt Carrie said. "Rental agents work long hours."

We looked at the directory in the lobby. His office was on the ninth floor. We followed Aunt Carrie into the elevator. I had read about them in my geography book, but it was the first time I had ever been on one. When the elevator boy closed the door I felt trapped and so did Dad—I could tell from the look in his eye.

There was nobody else on the elevator. We shot up like a jack-in-the-box, only we were still in the box. When he put on the brake, we caught up with ourselves. I was glad to get out and so was Dad. We walked along the corridor and stopped before a lighted door.

"Somebody's here," Aunt Carrie said, and opened the door. A man was bent over a desk, writing something in a book. He heard us and turned.

"This office is closed," he said.

"We've come to rent a house," Aunt Carrie said.

"That's different," the man said. "Where is it?"

"1921 Register Street."

The agent picked up another book and thumbed through it. "It's still vacant. How long do you intend to stay?"

"Until we can find a better place," Dad said.

The man looked at Dad. "In that case, you'll have to sign a year's lease."

"Do you want to do that, George?" Aunt Carrie asked.

"I don't like to sign papers, but it's the best we can do now." The agent took two printed forms and a piece of carbon paper. He slipped them into a typewriter and filled them out.

"Sign both and keep the carbon for yourself," he said.

Dad did read the contract before signing. "We can move in the first of July," he said.

"Since it's vacant, you can come a day or two early if you want," the agent said. "I'll be around to collect the rent the first of each month, beginning in August."

Dad gave him thirty dollars and the agent wrote a receipt. When we got back to our room, Dad wrote Mama a letter and sent her the receipt for the first month's rent.

"In a few days we will be getting home cooking again, son," he said. "My stomach is beginning to fail me." That didn't stop him from getting a sandwich and a cup of coffee before going to bed.

By the end of the first week, my arm had stopped aching. I wasn't carrying as much water as I had those first couple of days. Most of the workers in the shipyard were like that. There were three men to do every job that one good man could have done and nobody worked hard except the men who had just been hired. You could always tell a new man—he worked.

We put in only half a day Saturday. I got my first pay envelope with $33.60 in it. In one week I had made more than I had the whole summer working at the bank. But my room and board took $15 and $3.60 had to be saved for next week's streetcar fares. When we decided to go home on the train to see Mama, the round-trip ticket cost $6.60. That left me a five dollar bill and some change for my week's work—not including the money I had won in the crap game.

"It's not what you make, but what it costs you to live," Dad said. "A dollar goes three times as far on the river."

"A dollar is harder to get on the river," I said.

"It always adds up to the same thing," Dad said, as the Bullet carried us on the last mile to our town. "It's a struggle for poor folks to live, no matter where we are."

Mama was surprised to see us. "You look thin and pale, Noah," she said. "Are you eating right?"

"Sure, Mama," I said, "feel how hard the muscle of my right arm is."

"He's all right," Dad said. "How much do you think he made the first week?"

"Twenty-five dollars?"

"Tell her, son," Dad said.

"My pay envelope had $33.60 in it, Mama," I said. "But I've only got seven dollars left."

"You've been gambling," she said. "Blood will tell."

"It costs so much to live in the city, Evaline," Dad said. "Just his room and board costs fifteen dollars."

"I could feed all three of us a week on that," she said, "even with today's high prices."

"You'll have a chance soon," Dad said. "You got my letter?"

"Yes. Is the house also in South Baltimore? I hope not."

"It's in East Baltimore, close to Clifton Park," Dad said.

"It's also close to a dump," I added.

"Does it have marble steps?" Mama asked.

"There are pretty marble steps and a vestibule finished in tile—and a bathroom inside," Dad said.

"That's better than what we have here," Mama said.

"Dad leased it for a year, Mama," I said.

"I've been asking around about the best way to move our furniture," Mama said. "A wagon from the coal yard will put it aboard the *B. S. Ford* and you can hire somebody in Baltimore to meet the boat with a wagon and haul the furniture to the house."

"Carrie said she could get one of the lumber wagons where she works to meet the boat," Dad said. "July first comes on a Tuesday, so you can move on Monday."

That settled it.

The next morning after breakfast, me and Dad went down to the cove where his bateau was on the beach. The hot sun was already opening its seams.

"My old bateau won't live long if I leave her out of the water," he said.

We sat down on the sand and looked across the cove. A hard crab was swimming on top of the water. The old heron was fishing in the shallows off the point—just where he had fished ever since I could remember.

"Maybe the river made me lazy," Dad said, "but it's nice to be in a peaceful place again after a week in that madhouse where we are working."

"We can come back after the war is over, Dad," I said. "Maybe by that time we will have the money to buy a place for ourselves right on the river."

"If nothing happens," he said.

"You always say nothing ever happens to you," I said.

"Nothing ever happens to a river man as long as he stays on the river, where he belongs," Dad said. "But I've left the river."

"Think of all the money you are making," I said.

"There are more important things than money," he said. "The best way to ruin a gentle dog is to give him a fresh bone every day. Pretty soon, he's growling at everybody, thinking they want to steal his bones."

"You'll never be that way, Dad."

"Looking across the cove makes me want to go soft crabbing every day for a month or to climb down under the bridge drawer and sleep in the shade. The river is so pretty under the bridge, like a green eyeshade."

"We'll come back to it, Dad," I said.

"We're here," he said, "and if I stay by my old bateau much longer, nobody will be able to tear me away from her and the river. Let's go back to the house while we can."

I went to church with Mama, and Dad took a nap on the couch in the parlor, like he always had. The rest must have helped him. He didn't complain anymore and seemed contented on the train going back to Baltimore.

When I went to work Monday morning, there were five new water boys to take the place of those who had quit or been fired. One of the new boys approached me.

"How many buckets of water do we have to carry a day?" he asked.

"That all depends how smart you are, Bud," I said. "Of course, you new fellows have to carry more than us experienced workers."

"Thank you," the new boy said. I knew he was going to have

trouble and wouldn't last long. Politeness may be important in a bank, but in a shipyard you need something else. Three men fell from the ships that morning; the siren on the ambulance shrieked three times. More men get hurt Monday in the shipyard than for all of the rest of the week put together.

The second week was like the first, but me and Dad were looking forward to having a house with Mama in it to live in. After working all day, we spent the evenings cleaning the worst of the dirt out of the house on Register Street. Mama would clean it all over again, but getting the worst would make it easier for her. One evening we walked over to the swimming pool in Clifton Park. It was larger than Brewster's Cove with hundreds of folks splashing around in it. Aunt Carrie was with us.

"It don't seem the same without an old crane or shitepoke standing fishing," Dad said. "You reckon there are any fish or crabs in it?"

"Of course not," Aunt Carrie said.

"There's a rowboat," I said, pointing to a small skiff with two men wearing jerseys with "Life Guard" written on them. They had a deep tan.

"The life guards have classes to teach you to swim," Aunt Carrie said. "You can learn the latest strokes like the Australian crawl."

That sounded good to me. Imagine saying to Ric, "Come on out to the draw, Ric, and I'll show you how to swim the Australian crawl." I would dive off a piling and swim away faster than a hard crab when you miss it with your dip net. Then I remembered that Ric might already be in France—I might never see him again.

The day Mama arrived on the *B. S. Ford* with our furniture, Aunt Carrie met the boat during her lunch hour. We went to the house on Register Street directly from the shipyard. It took half an hour more on the streetcars. The last one we boarded carried a number 13, and Dad didn't like to ride on it. But when we finally came to the street it was worth it—we could smell Mama's meat cakes halfway down the block.

"It's good to be coming home from work to home cooking," Dad said.

The marble front steps were so white I thought we were at the wrong house. "Your mother has scrubbed them again," Dad said.

The front door was locked. "I'll ring the bell and scare her," Dad said, pushing the button.

Mama opened the door a crack until she saw it was us. "I've been waiting supper since six o'clock for you," she said, "and beginning to think you had been in a streetcar accident."

"It's a two-hour ride from the shipyard home, Evaline," Dad said. "How do you like the house?"

"It'll do until we can get a better one," Mama said. "We've got helpful neighbors; they've been helping me move the furniture all afternoon. Good neighbors are more important than good houses."

After supper, I sat on the front steps; they faced the dump instead of the park. Mama sat in the parlor, rocking, and I heard the springs of the couch squeak and knew that Dad was resting.

"Mother," my father said softly, "we're sure glad you are here with us, but there's more to it than that. This war's changing Noah from a soft crab to a hard shell."

"George, stop comparing Noah to river things; he'll never follow the river," Mama replied just as softly.

Then the moon came up, right out of the dump instead of the river—it was full and yellow. Two houses away, a girl came out and sat on the front steps. The moon shone on her yellow curls. We looked at one another and then we looked the other way.

The next morning when we got to the shipyard, there were two more new water boys. I often wondered why there were so many new water boys. By mid-August, I was the only one left from the fellows who were working there when I started.

In August, it got awfully hot in the afternoons, and one day I was so sleepy it was hard to keep my eyes open. The foreman had already checked me for ten buckets of water, so I started looking for a good place to take a nap. I sort of drifted away from the ships and slipped in between two piles of lumber. It was out of the sun, and a breeze drifted through the tunnel made by the lumber. I stretched out on a board and went to sleep.

I was dreaming of the river, and walking along with my dip net and found a hole filled with quarters. I was picking up the money when a giant crab seized me with his big fighting claws. When I opened my eyes, the foreman of the water boys was shaking me.

"Sleeping on the job," he said. "You're the fifth boy I've caught sleeping this week. You're fired. Go over to the pay-master's office and get your pay, then get out of here."

"Yes, sir," I said, and handed him my bucket.

"And don't come back," he said. He looked awfully tired. He needed to take a nap, but bosses never get to snooze awhile.

I had to wait outside the gate. Dad had a hard time finding me.

"I was worried about you," he said.

"I've been fired," I said.

"What for?"

"My boss caught me taking a nap."

"You needed a vacation before going back to school," he said.

"You'll have time to learn to swim the Australian crawl at the park."

Mama didn't like it when she learned that I had lost my job.

"We needed that extra money to help pay your expenses at the preparatory school," she said.

"I'm getting a raise of ten cents an hour next week," Dad said. "We'll make out all right."

"Noah needs money for a new suit," Mama said.

Dad peeled two twenty dollar bills from his roll. "Take this and stop worrying," he said.

"You've been gambling again, George," Mama said, but she took the money.

I had a two-week vacation and talked to the girl who lived two doors from us. Her name was Cecilia, but I didn't learn to swim the Australian crawl.

When the tailor at the clothing store measured me for a new suit, he was surprised.

"What have you been doing to yourself, Bud?" he asked. "Your right shoulder sags two inches."

19

🐚 Meet the Pope

"**Y**our *father and I* want you to have a better chance than we had, Noah," Mama said as she packed my trunk. "If you get enough education you'll be able to wear a white collar every day and live like a gentleman."

I remembered what Grandpappy had said about Mr. Eben Pauley and how he got to be president of the bank. "Miss Fannie used to tell us that it takes three generations to make a gentleman, Mama," I said.

Dad was resting on the couch. "That's not the way I heard it," he said. "Miss Fannie gave you the English idea. In this country, it takes three generations from shirt sleeves to shirt sleeves."

"What's that got to do with it?" Mama said.

"What d'you mean, Dad?" I asked.

"You'll know what it means by the time you're my age," he said. "You're caught in the middle."

"You're talking crazy, George," Mama said. "Why don't you go back to sleep?"

The next day I boarded the *B. S. Ford* and the side-wheeler ran across the bay and up the Chester River to my home town with its college on the hill. George Washington gave fifty guineas toward the establishment of the college and received an honorary degree at its first commencement. That's what it says in the college's catalogue.

When a fellow is old enough to go away to school, he can go anywhere he wants to on the *Ford*. I hung around the bar on the lower deck for a while, watching a poker game.

"Don't you look at my cards, boy," one of the players said to me. "My luck is bad enough without having you Jonahing me."

"You're George's boy, ain't you?" another player said, and I recognized Charley who used to sail with Captain Pete.

"Hello, Mr. Charley," I said.

"I heard you folks had moved to Baltimore," he said. "You coming down for a visit?"

"I'm entering the preparatory school at the college," I said.

"Flying sort of high, ain't you," he said, "now that your pop is working steady."

"It was mostly Mama's idea."

"I was slated for the army, but the docs turned me down because of my flat feet," he said. "Flat feet are just fine on a muddy bottom, but the army don't like them."

I left the poker game and climbed the steps to the main cabin. I picked out a red plush chair and put my suitcase beside it. That reserved the chair for me in case I wanted to walk around the boat. I sat down and took out a pair of amber dice I bought at a cigar store. The red plush carpet was just the place to roll them.

"Where'd you get those dice, Buddy?" a voice said, and I slipped them quickly into my pocket. But it was only a fellow about my age, although he was much taller than me. I hadn't heard him walking on the thick carpet.

"I bought them in Baltimore," I said, taking them out of my pocket.

He took the dice and held them up to the light. "Are they loaded?"

"No."

"Where are you going?" he asked.

"I'm entering the preparatory school at the college."

"So am I," he said. "My name is Owen Thomas; I'm from Rockville."

"I'm Noah Marlin from Baltimore," I said.

"Are you prepared to meet your Maker?" he asked.

"What's that?" I said, thinking I had heard him wrong.

"Seeing you with the dice made me wonder," he said. "Don't you know they are the tools of the devil?"

"Are you studying for the ministry?" I asked.

He laughed. "I was just kidding. Let's go down to the men's room and make a few passes."

On the way he asked me what my nickname was.

I hesitated before telling him. "The fellows where I worked at the shipyard called me Hungry."

"Hungry," he said, looking at me. "That fits, you do have sort of a hungry look. The fellows call me Pope."

It was easy to see why he was called Pope. He had a pompous way about him that only faded when he grinned. Then he looked like one of the griffins on the fountain in the town square.

The men's room was empty so we rolled the dice against the wall, but we didn't put any money on the floor. There's no telling who will come into a men's room.

"You ever play Put and Take, Hungry?" Pope asked.

"I don't think so," I said, as he brought a small top out of his pocket. It was an octagon and marked differently on each side.

"You have to do what the top says," Pope explained. "Do you want to play?"

"I'm lucky," I said. "I might win all your money and you wouldn't like that."

"Let's play just for fun," Pope said, so I put the dice away. Pope spun the top. When it stopped it read, "Put a quarter."

"I've always been unlucky gambling," Pope said.

"I almost always win," I said, spinning the top. It read, "Take a quarter."

"You know what they say, 'Lucky at cards, unlucky at love,'" Pope said. "What's your girl's name, Hungry?"

"I don't have a girl," I said.

"You must have a girl somewhere," Pope said.

I thought of Dora Tilghman, but she was more Ric's girl than mine, and I thought of the girl who sat on the white marble steps, near our house on Register Street.

"There's a city girl who lives near me," I said. "Her yellow hair is pretty in the moonlight." I didn't mention the dump. "What's your girl like?"

"She's tall and slender, with black hair and brown eyes and a soft voice, like velvet," Pope said. "Only I've never seen her."

"You haven't seen her?"

"She's my dream girl," Pope said, "like the one in the song. The girls don't like me, so I dream of one instead. Do the girls like you?"

"I think so," I said, "but they sort of scare me."

"Who are you rooming with?" Pope asked.

"I was to get a roommate after getting there."

"So was I. Let's room together," Pope said.

We shook hands on it. I had made a new friend even though Pope was a lot different from me. Later I learned his father was an Episcopal clergyman.

"Do you get hungry, Hungry?" Pope asked with a grin.

"I'm starved now," I said. "Let's get a hot dog and something to drink."

"Let's get a bottle of beer," Pope said.

"I've never drunk beer," I said.

"Me neither," Pope said, "but we can get a big bottle of root beer for a nickel. It looks like the real thing with suds on top of the mugs."

We drank the root beer to wash down a couple of hot dogs dressed with lots of mustard and chopped pickles before going back to the main cabin.

Pope took out a pack of Little Recruits and offered me one. "They're almost as good as a cigar," he said, as we lit up and puffed away.

"I like Sweet Caporals," I said, thinking that the brown to-bacco-wrapped Little Recruits seemed awfully strong.

"Did you ever smoke a Mexican cigarette?" Pope asked. "They taste like a piece of rope."

"Do you inhale?" I asked, letting the smoke come out of my nose.

"Sure," he said and swallowed a big puff. Pope almost choked and started coughing. "Let's see you inhale, Hungry," he said, gasping for air.

I didn't swallow much but it was too much and it stayed down in my lungs. My stomach felt funny and I had an awful taste in my mouth. I was giddy.

"That beer we had on the lower deck was awfully strong, Pope," I said.

"It did have a big head on it," he said. "Don't you feel well?"

"Not too good, Pope," I said. "Maybe the hot dogs were spoiled."

The *B. S. Ford* ploughed into a big bay wave and rolled. "I don't feel too good, myself," Pope said. "Let's go out on deck and get some fresh air."

The salt air was bracing, but it wasn't pleasant to watch the *Ford*'s bow rise and fall as it hit the large waves.

"Let's go inside again," Pope said, so we stretched out in the big red plush chairs, and as the steamboat moved into the quieter waters of the Chester River, I dozed off. Every time the steamboat blew for a landing, I awoke, and listened to the sounds as the boat was unloaded and loaded, but it was too much trouble to go out on deck. My insides had quieted down and I didn't want to stir them up again. Pope must have felt the same way. The rush of the water against the paddle wheels made us want to sleep and sleep. Past Queenstown, a tall, thin colored man wearing a white coat and ringing a bell walked through the cabin.

"Dinner is served in the dining salon," he called. "Dinner is now being served in the dining salon."

Pope awoke and sat up. "Are you hungry, Hungry?"

"Mama packed me a lunch," I said, opening the shoe box.

There was enough for both of us, and while I was opening it, Pope went down to the lower deck and bought some candy bars. We decided to drink water instead of root beer. After finishing our meal, we went out on deck again.

Now we could see the water tank that stands on the hill by the college.

"There's writing on it," Pope said, straining his eyes to read it.

"The college football team beat St. John's College a couple of years ago," I said. "Some of the college fellows painted the score, 27-7, on the tank."

"That's great," Pope said. "Let's climb the tank together."

"It's 150 feet to the bell," I said. "I don't like to climb that much."

"You mean you're yellow?" Pope said.

"Wait until you see the ladder you have to climb," I said. "In some places, it leans backward. You'd be yellow, too."

"I can't wait," Pope said.

"We'll be docking in ten minutes," I said. "Let's move our baggage so we'll be first across the gangplank."

"How far is it from the wharf to the college?" Pope asked.

"It's about a mile and a half and the last part of the walk is uphill," I said.

"My suitcase weighs a ton," Pope said. "Won't there be any hacks at the wharf?"

"Old Simon from the hotel will be there, only he charges a quarter if you're not going to the Voshell House."

"What's a quarter?" Pope said. "It's important how you go to a place. Let's ride."

"It's O.K. with me," I said. When the B.S. *Ford* docked, we hurried across the gangplank and were the first to get into the hack marked *Voshell House*.

"You young gentlemen going to the hotel?" Simon asked.

"We want to be taken to the college, Simon," I said.

When I called him by name, he looked at me more closely. "I didn't know you Mr. Noah, you've grown so, and with those city clothes."

A couple of drummers with their sample cases climbed in beside us. Simon slapped the two horses with the reins as the hack gathered speed to make the hill that led away from the wharf. We clattered along Main Street and stopped at the hotel. Simon helped the salesmen with their luggage and mounted the driver's seat again.

"Where do you young gentlemen want to go at the college?" he asked.

Pope turned to me. "The catalogue says the preparatory boys room in Middle Hall," I said.

"Middle Hall," Pope said.

"Yes, sir," Simon said and touched up his horses. Soon we were climbing the hill that leads to the college. The sun was low—its slants struck the long row of maples that line College Avenue. Even so early in September a few leaves were turning to gold. The red pavement bricks framed the maples and the rolling green campus. In the distance the red brick buildings looked like doll houses. I was glad we had decided to ride to the college.

At the top of the hill, Simon turned left and the horses climbed a steep grade before stopping at the middle one of three dormitories. Pope and I got out with our suitcases.

There must have been fifteen fellows sitting on the steps to Middle Hall, smoking and talking.

"Look at that rig the small one is wearing," a big fellow said. He was smoking a big pipe with a curved stem.

"The tall boy looks like a preacher," a smaller chap said.

"Is this Middle Hall?" Pope asked, just for something to say.

"That is what it is generally called," the big fellow with the pipe said.

"Fire," somebody yelled from a window above, and the fellows on the steps put their hands over their heads and ducked. We newcomers looked up to see where the fire was, and a paper bag full of water just missed us. It broke on the brick walk and gave us both a showerbath.

The big fellow with the pipe rose and bowed. "Welcome to Washington College, new men," he said. "We all hope that your stay here will be pleasant. I assure you that such outrages as the one just perpetrated will not occur more than once each hour. Now give us your names."

"Owen Thomas," Pope said.

"We don't care about your baptismal name, fellow," the big chap said. "What's your nickname?"

"Pope."

All of the fellows on the steps laughed.

"That fits," the big fellow said. "From now on you will be known as the Pope."

"Amen!" the others sang, holding it longer than we did in the church choir.

The big fellow turned to me. "What's your nickname, boy?"

I didn't know whether to tell him or not.

"Go ahead and tell him," Pope whispered.

"Hungry," I said, not very loud.

"What's that?" the big fellow said.

"Hungry," I said, louder.

All of the fellows on the steps hooted and my face turned red.

"You do have a hungry look," the big fellow said. "From now on you shall be called the Hungry One."

"Amen," they all sang and for some reason it meant more now than it ever had in church. It reminded me of the day I had been confirmed and the bishop had traced the cross on my forehead with holy water. I had a happy feeling inside. Even if I was to be known as the Hungry One, at least I was one and belonged.

The supper bell began to ring and the fellows on the steps ran toward the dining hall, which was in the basement of the East Hall. We followed them. But the doors to the dining room were locked with all of the college boys milling around outside and complaining.

"Why do they ring the bell and still keep the doors locked?" the big fellow asked.

"Don't you remember reading about Pavlov's experiments with dogs and their saliva glands?" a tall boy who wore thick glasses said. "They're using us in place of the dogs."

"We ought to break down the door," the big fellow said, and gave the paneling a few kicks. "Open up."

"Grease your tail and slide under," a voice said on the other side of the door.

"That was Tick Green, one of the scholarship waiters," the fellow with the glasses said. "He's too smart for a freshman."

Then we heard the bolts slide back and the door popped open.

"Seniors!" the big fellow shouted, and a group of the older men disappeared through the door.

"Juniors!" a tall boy called, and other older fellows moved toward their food.

"Sophomores!" came from a younger group.

"Freshmen," a boy with a pimply face said, as if he wasn't certain, and a large gang of new men slipped through the opening.

"Second Prep," a boy standing beside Pope called, and those who were left ran through the door.

Pope and I looked at one another. "First Prep!" we sang, and crept to our suppers.

During supper, one of the fellows at our table told us where Dr. Hull, the registrar, lived. He also had charge of assigning the rooms in the dormitories. Pope and I went over to his house to see about rooming together.

Dr. Hull answered the door bell and took us into his study where there were more books than I have ever seen in one room before—even more than in the town library. After we gave him our names, he consulted several large charts on his desk.

"You boys are both rooming on the third floor of Middle Hall," he said, "but you won't be together. Nelson Wheelock of Westminster is your roommate, Noah. John Compton from St. Mary's County will room with you, Owen."

We both tried to get Dr. Hull to change his chart so we could room together but it wasn't any use.

"Your roommates have already occupied their rooms," he said. "You're both on the same floor. You'll see plenty of each other."

He gave us the keys to our rooms and we returned to Middle Hall. It was a long climb to the third floor carrying our heavy suitcases. When I got to the room, my trunk was already there. It had been shipped by express the day before.

Sitting at a table was my roommate, Nelson Wheelock. He was older and larger than me and was smoking a pipe while reading the sports page of the daily newspaper. He had protected his eyes with a green shade. He put down the newspaper when he saw me.

"You must be Noah," he said.

"That's right," I said, "and you're Nelson."

"My friends call me Cobb," he said. "Ty has been my hero for years. He got four hits yesterday and drove in three runs to beat the Yankees almost single-handed. Now he's batting .375. What's your nickname?"

"A lot of fellows call me Hungry," I said.

"Do you like it?"

"Not much."

"I'll just call you 'kid' until I can think of a better name," Cobb said.

20

🐦 Bird on Wing

M*ama wrote to me* every week and always enclosed a dollar bill for spending money. If I delayed answering one of her letters, she would write again, asking if I was sick and enclosing a stamp to mail my answer. Then one day in late October, when I opened her letter, a ten dollar bill was enclosed. Maybe Dad has had a big raise, I thought, and read:

> Dear Noah,
> Your father has been hurt at the shipyard and is now in Mercy Hospital. The crane dropped a load of lumber and one piece hit your father's leg, breaking it in several places. He is as well as can be expected, and cheerful, but keeps asking for you. I am sending you ten dollars so you can come home to see him as soon as possible.
>
> Love,
> Mama

The letter didn't seem real. I read it again, still holding the ten dollar bill. Cobb saw it.

"Flashing something big, aren't you, kid?" he said.

"Dad has been hurt, Cobb," I said.

"Hurt?"

"In the shipyard, a timber fell on his leg."

"Maybe he's just broken his leg," Cobb said. "I had my leg broken once by a fallen tree. I was all right again in a couple of months."

"Maybe that's all," I said, but I thought of those huge cranes that carried timbers weighing more than a ton. "I'm going home to see Dad. He's in the hospital."

"Sure, kid," Cobb said. "That's the thing to do."

The dean gave me permission and I left the next day on the *B. S. Ford*. We passed a couple of bateaus like Dad's on the upper river, and near the mouth of the Chester there were a lot of oyster tongers in their log canoes and bateaus. Hundreds of wild geese and ducks were feeding in the shallows close to the shore. I thought of how Dad used to say: "Nothing happens to a river man as long as he stays on the river, where he belongs."

When the *Ford* docked on Light Street, I went to the house on Register Street. Mama was all dressed up like it was Sunday; she had just come home from the hospital.

"How's Dad?" I asked.

"He's getting used to the hospital, and not afraid of it now," she said. "They're doing everything they can for him. The shipyard pays all the expenses."

"How bad is he hurt, Mama?" I asked.

"The doctors say his leg has a compound fracture. Carrie says that means it's crushed. They've fastened the bones together with a silver plate and put his leg in a plaster paris cast."

"Will he ever be able to walk again?" I asked.

"Lord knows," she said. "It's too soon for the doctors to say. Have you had your dinner?"

"No, ma'am."

"You sit down and rest while I put some food on the table. Then you'll feel better."

That night the two of us went to see Dad. He was propped up in bed smoking a cigarette and reading a magazine.

"Hello, Dad," I said, and kissed his cheek like I used to when I was a small boy.

"Hello, son," he said, smiling.

"How are they treating you, George?" Mama asked. "Did they give you a good supper?"

"It's not home cooking, but the nurse said it was nourishing."

I could see Dad's bad leg, bulging under the covers as big as a log.

"How's your leg feel, Dad?" I asked.

"It don't hurt so much during the daytime. The doc said today he'd take the cast off in a couple of weeks."

"I'm going to see the doctor, now," Mama said. "You stay with your father, Noah."

"How'd you come over, Noah?" asked Dad.

"On the *Ford*."

"Were they taking many oysters?"

"I counted fifty tong boats in the mouth of the Chester. The wild geese and ducks are back again."

"Didn't you see the *Kessie Price*?"

"No, sir. I heard in town that Captain Pete is laid up with rheumatism and can hardly walk."

"Me and him both," Dad said. "How do you like it at the prep school?"

"I like it," I said, and told him about my older professors.

He laughed. "Mind you the time we passed Dr. Mike's speedboat in my old bateau? How is my old girl?"

"She's right where you left her. Her seams are opening up."

"An old boat can't live long out of the water. If I ever get on my two feet again, I'll go back to her—if I have to walk all the way." He moved his leg that was in the cast. "See, I can move it now."

"You'll be back on the river come spring, Dad," I said.

"Maybe so. I knew all along I should have never left it. The Chester River is as much a part of me as the blood that flows through my veins." He winced like his leg might have been hurting him. "If I could only get my poor leg in the river—that would soon heal it."

Mama came back. "The doctor can't tell a thing about your leg until the cast is taken off, and that will be two weeks. These city doctors are not like Doctor Salmons. He'll take the time to sit down and comfort you."

"I certainly would like to have a mess of your oyster fritters, Evaline," Dad said.

"Sounds like you are getting better, George, thinking about your stomach."

"I'm just getting used to things," he said.

The bell ending visiting hours rang so we had to go.

"We'll be back to see you tomorrow, Dad," I said, as I kissed him good-bye.

Mama was sick after we got home. All the excitement of Dad's accident finally caught up with her. Aunt Carrie got my supper. The next day, Mama had a bad headache, so I went alone to see Dad.

"Where's your mother?" he asked right away.

"She's not feeling so good and stayed home today, Dad."

"She's been to see me every day since I was hurt," he said. "A day off will do her good."

"How are you feeling, today, Dad?" I asked.

"I'm sort of feverish. My leg feels like it is swelling inside the cast."

"What does the doctor say?"

"He says it's to be expected, whatever that means. How's your school work going?"

"All right, Dad. I don't have any trouble with the books."

"You wouldn't. Are you happy?"

"Most of the time."

"What do you mean?"

"Yesterday, when I saw all the tongers in the Chester, for a while I wondered if I was missing something."

"Since hurting my leg, I've had plenty of time to think things over, boy. Your mother has been right all the time—it's best you forget all about the river. With a college education, you make more money easier ashore—and you'll live more comfortably and respectably wearing a white collar every day."

I'd never heard Dad talk like that before. It worried me. I wondered if he was giving up.

"I was dreaming of sailing the *Kessie Price* and not watching the crane when it dropped the timbers," he continued. "The next thing I knew here I was stretched out on this hospital cot. You'd better forget all about the river; even thinking about her will get you into trouble."

"When I make enough money, I'll buy a cruising sailboat and follow the water on weekends and vacations," I said. "You can sail with me, Dad."

"You're not listening to me," he said. "Forget it. Folks are always calling our bailiwick a paradise. It's a paradise all right—a paradise for fools."

Dad's eyes were bright with fever. "I'd better be going now," I said.

"Are you coming to see me tomorrow, boy?" he asked.

"I've got to get back to school to be ready for Monday's classes," I said, "but it won't be very long to Thanksgiving. I'll see you then."

The next day, on the B. S. *Ford*, I sat in one of the big chairs in the main cabin and tried to figure things out. I wondered if Dad would ever get back to the river again and if I really wanted to leave it so as to wear a white collar every day. The big chair confined me so I went out on the top deck.

It was a warm, sunny day in late October with a southwest wind. Twenty skipjacks and three of the larger bugeyes were dredging the oyster bars off Kent Island. When we entered the mouth of the Chester River, the tong boats were as thick as the rafts of wild geese and whistling swans. A log sailing canoe, low in the water with its load of oysters, raced past us on its way home. One of the tongers had his hand on the tiller; the other man was culling the oysters.

I wondered if I would ever discover anything in a book to take the place of the sight of this Chesapeake Bay log sailing canoe and its crew running toward home with a fair breeze.

But I was glad to see Cobb and Pope and the other fellows, even Gravy Bronson. On Monday, we had an algebra assignment about combinations. It had to do with possibilities.

"Is it possible to calculate the chances of throwing a seven with a pair of dice, Doctor?" Pope asked.

"It is possible, but I've never worked out the formula," Sprig said. "How do you play this game called 'craps,' Mr. Thomas?"

"I don't exactly know, Doctor," Pope said. "I play poker—it's more educational."

We all roared except Sprig. He didn't think it was funny.

"Don't forget, gentlemen, the faculty recently enacted a strict regulation forbidding all gambling."

"But our whole life is a gamble, Doctor," Cobb said. "My father is a farmer; he gambles every day with the weather."

"Just the same, if any student is apprehended while gambling, you will be suspended for two weeks. A second offense will be punished by expulsion."

If the faculty ever enforced that rule, the college would have to close its doors. It was the war, with death waiting for us when we became old enough to be drafted, that had increased gambling everywhere.

I gathered from Mama's letters that Dad's leg wasn't any better. I wrote him a letter and he answered, short and to the point. He had just finished reading *Huckleberry Finn.* Mama was getting him other books from the public library. He had plenty of time to read, he said.

Soon it was time for the Thanksgiving holiday and I was in Baltimore again. When I visited Dad, the cast had been removed from his leg, but he was worse. His leg was hoisted; there were tubes and a sickly odor.

"Hello, Dad," I said. When I kissed his cheek it was burning with fever.

"It's Noah," he said. His eyes were red with fever.

"Read any more books by Mark Twain, Dad?" I asked.

"I haven't read much for the last few days," he said. "I've been feverish." He was thinner than I had ever seen him, but he hadn't given up. "Did you see the *Kessie Price* on your way to Baltimore, son?"

"No, I didn't, Dad. It was a rough day, the wind northwest and really blowing—not many dredge boats were working."

"It's funny, every once in a while it seems I hear the *Kessie Price* blowing." An automobile on the street below tooted its horn. "Hear that, there it is again."

"That's an auto horn, Dad," I said.

"So the nurse told me, but it sounds like Captain Pete blowing for the bridge. Once I tried to get out of bed, but the nurse stopped me."

Dad was more than feverish, thinking that Captain Pete and the *Kessie Price* were sailing down a city street. He was almost out of his head with fever.

When I went home I told Mama.

"He's getting worse all the time, Noah," she said. "The poison in his leg is spreading through his whole body."

"Can't the doctors do anything?" I asked.

"Day before yesterday, the doctor told me it was too late to amputate. The poison has already spread. He may get better and he may get worse. All we can do is pray."

Sunday, I went back to school. Several of the fellows were on the boat—we played poker during most of the trip. I heard someone standing in back of my chair, and turning, I saw it was Captain Pete. He was crippled with rheumatism and carrying a full load of liquor.

"Hello, Captain Pete," I said.

"Hello, boy, how's your pop? I'd have gone to see him yesterday, but I'm scared to death of hospitals. It would take a team of horses to drag me into one."

I told him how Dad was.

"He should have never left the river," Captain Pete said. "He took a big chance and now he's lost. Where are you going?"

"Back to prep school."

"So your mother got her way, did she? That's a mistake, too. You've got too much of the river in you to ever go far with books. Look what you're going to miss, cooped up reading a book or adding figures. When you get your fill of it, look me up. You'll make a good schooner-man."

"Yes, sir," I said, not wanting to argue with him, but down deep inside of me I knew that Dad and I had left the river for good—we would never follow the water again.

Done Crabbin'

Designed by Ann Walston

Composed by Blue Heron
in Goudy Old Style text and display

Printed by R.R. Donnelley & Sons Company
on 55-lb. S.D. Warren's Cream White Sebago,
and bound in Joanna Arrestox and G.S.B.
with James River Papan end sheets

Library of Congress Cataloging-in-Publication Data

Byron, Gilbert.
   Done crabbin' : Noah leaves the river / Gilbert Byron.
       p.   cm.
   Sequel to: The Lord's oysters.
   ISBN 0-8018-3988-2 (alk. paper)
   1. Chesapeake Bay Region (Md. and Va.)—Fiction.
   2. Eastern Shore (Md. and Va.)—Fiction. 3. Fishers—
   Fiction. I. Title.
PS3503.Y95D6   1990
813'.54—dc20   89-27556 CIP